PERRI'S GATES

LORNA HOPKINS KEITH

DEDICATION

To my husband Greg, who supported me through thick and thin.

APPRECIATION

Thanks again to my Wordsmiths' writers' group, for picking this apart so I could put it together properly.

TABLE OF CONTENTS

Copyright
Dedication
Appreciation

PART ONE – THE GATE

PART TWO – OTHER WORLDS

PART THREE – ALIENS

PART ONE – THE GATE

Chapter 1   A New Talent

As my brother and I trotted down the tree lined trail from the ridge above River Point on Harmony, the spring breeze tousled our curls. I delighted in this wonderful day of freedom of the others.

Down below, I saw Neela chasing little Cam up the trail. At the curve around the huge boulder, Cam ran straight across the rock to the far edge.

From five paces up the trail, well above Neela and her toddler, I *caught* him as he stepped off the boulder. I dropped him, squalling, at his mother's feet, and gasped.

'No,' I cried inside my head, shaking. What was happening to me, to my Talent?

Neela picked up the baby and whirled around. "What did you do? Leave us be," she screamed, and ran down the trail.

I took a couple of hesitating steps. I'd never done any kind of teleportation before. What was going on with my Talent?

"Nice catch, Perri," my twin, Peter, said, coming down behind me. I only heard him inside my head.

"Oh shut up. I didn't do it on purpose, it just happened." I was still shaking, arms wrapped around myself.

"Oh sure. Right. It just came out of nowhere."

"Just stuff it, little brother. Did you hear what she said? My name's mud, now. It's bad enough we can communicate in our minds, but how will they accept that I can move people?" *If I could do that, what else could I do?*

"Calm down, sis. Maybe it was a onetime thing."

I turned and looked up at him. Up. He'd never been taller than me, until this last year. *Life at sixteen was getting scary in many ways.* "At least you don't have to deal with people, only things."

"People get mad when I mess up their things, or break them. How did you get all the people Talent anyway?"

"I was born first. Go away and bother someone else."

"You know I can't, I have to stay with you until we get back."

"I don't care." I ran on down the trail, in between the trees bright with new leaves. I wasn't just scared, I was terrified. Communicating with the family in my mind was okay, it was the only way I could hear, something in my ears didn't work. The others mostly accepted that, but this? And we were too small a colony here on Harmony to split up.

I ran past the cut off to the cabin, around a sharp curve, and into Mama. Literally. She caught me. "Watch where you're going. Where's Peter?" She *sent* it to my mind as well as saying it out loud.

"Back there." I pushed her away to look at her square face, green eyes and black curls. Everyone says I look just like her. "Mama, my Talent's going crazy. Neela's baby was falling and I caught him and put him in front of her, without touching him at all. I wasn't even anywhere near them, and I did it without knowing I was going to. What's happening to me?"

"How far away were you?"

"I don't know. Ten feet?"

"It must have been instinctive." She took me into her arms. The shaking stopped, I was safe with her. "This Talent can be a pain at times. There was a cousin back on Earth, I saw things I never should have. We just have to learn to live with it, and yes, I'm still learning, too."

"But you never did anything like what I did." I laid my forehead on her shoulder.

"No, but your Talent is stronger than mine. And the Bramites will never understand this." She looked behind me. "Hello, Peter, did you get lost?"

"No, Mama," he said, coming up to us and patting my shoulder. Mama let me go. "She really was scared, and I thought it best to let her run. I knew where she was all the time."

Because the only way I could hear was through a mindlink with a member of the family, Peter was supposed to stay with me all the time when we were out together.

"And I see you didn't help much," Mama said, *touching* his mind. "Come on, you two."

We followed her back to our cabin, higher on the hillside than the others.

"The pump isn't working right again, Peter. See what you can do." Mama dumped her bag of school papers and went into the kitchen.

I plopped down on the old brown couch and caught my breath. I was safe here, I thought. But that feeling didn't last long. Mama came back and said we needed vegetables. "Let's go down and see what's in the warehouse."

"I'd rather stay here." I was afraid to face anyone else now. Papa would be home soon.

"I need you to help carry things back," Mama said as she gathered up a couple of empty bags. Reluctantly I followed her out the door and down the hill to the storehouse by the plaza.

"Mama, is there any way to get rid of the Talent?" I asked as I caught up to her.

"Why would you want to do that?"

"It scares me and makes me different from the other girls."

"Have they been saying anything?"

"Not really." I couldn't explain what I'd felt. "Just a feeling."

"Well, to answer your question, no, we can't do anything about it, we just have to live with it. None of us chose to have Talent. It's just part of our Harlan heritage, from my father, your grandfather, his father and on back, all thanks to the Watchers. We all have to learn to use it for our own good."

I mumbled something as I caught a glimpse of the river below.

"But if you want to know what it would be like without it." She stopped. My world went silent as she *shielded* my mindlink, and I lost my connection to everyone.

I turned and said, "Mama," hearing it only in my mind. Mama just smiled at me, motionless. I couldn't *find* anyone else. A tree branch in front of me moved and I jumped. Everything looked flat, like a picture. The world was no longer real. "No," I cried.

Mama closed her eyes and opened them. The world came back. "Okay," I said. "I guess I'll have to live with it."

"You can do it. There was a woman on Earth, who lived before I did, who was born without hearing, like you, but she was also blind. She eventually learned how to speak and write. You can handle this. Let's go."

We moved on.

I thought of our Talents, given us by the Watchers, a no longer physical people, who had been breeding our ancestors for a race to replace them. None of us liked the idea, but there was nothing we could do about it. Yet.

Twelve people had come here from Earth. Mama, Papa, and all the cousins they could find considering the anti-science atmosphere in the United States. Plus Uncle Adam, Mama's half-brother, from Ruthor. A couple hundred of the Bramites, all that was left of their colony on Brama, had come with us, on the Wati ship, Emprisa. The Wati were another oppressed people, their world being taken over by Centar, the rulers of that part of the galaxy. That was about twenty years ago, and our settlements had prospered and grown.

We reached the plaza, surrounded by the brown brick meeting house, workshops, storehouse, medical clinic, and school. While Mama went to pick out veggies, I walked down to the river overlook at the bottom of the plaza. Faint fragrance from blossoming fruit trees spiced the air. The river ambled along, and the fields beyond were speckled with green sprouts. A hen pecked at my feet.

I tried to move her with my mind, but nothing happened. Maybe it was a onetime thing.

"Hello," Uncle Adam said, appearing at my side. He had the same square face, black curls and wide eyes that we had.

"Oh hi, Uncle Adam. Anything new?" I hadn't seen him for a couple of days.

"Not much." He smiled down at me. "We are getting kind of crowded here. How do you feel about opening up a new settlement?"

"A new settlement?" I looked at him. People had been talking about it. "Really? Where? I guess we could use it when my year people start bonding and having babies." I wasn't quite ready to think about that yet.

"The council is considering a few locations. Most likely at the north river."

"Considering what?" Mama asked, arms full. She handed me a bag of vegetables.

"A new settlement up north," I said.

"No." Mama stomped her foot. "There's not enough of us to split up. But there's another problem, Adam. One of the boys in my last class, son of woodcutters, said his grandfather says there's some kind of bug in the trees, making them no good for building."

"I'll talk to Emek." Uncle Adam nodded. Mama sent us the details by mindlink. Emek was the Bramites' leader. "But, Lyn, we do need to look for sites for future settlements. People are complaining about crowding now, and with another bonding coming up, it'll only get worse. And the river can support only so many. We need to at least start preparing now."

"No." Mama crossed her arms, bag dangling.

"I realize it would be better for us all to stay together for another five to ten years, but we may not have that choice in another year or so," Uncle Adam said. "The people prefer the flat land along the river and that is as full as we dare have it. Emek says many of the young people from the last bonding want a new place. He and I want to send Allen up with an exploration team to scout out the north river site."

Mama sighed. "Just to see if it is at all possible," she said. I knew she had a fear of her people being divided, even though we could stay in contact with our Talent. "But two days' walk is just too far," she added.

I knew that Charley, my future mate, wanted to move to a new place when we were bonded. Peter would have to wait another year, his Anne was too young yet, but he'd want to be close to me.

Mama sighed again, and shifted her bag to her other arm. "I do see your point, Adam, but something about it bothers me. Something about Perri."

"Me?"

"Yes, dear. But I can't pinpoint what."

Peter trotted down to us. "Did you hear what Perri did?" he asked Uncle Adam.

"Yes, dear," Mama said. "I know all about it. It's been discussed and dealt with."

"What is this?" Uncle Adam asked.

"Tell him."

I gave him a brief description.

"Has this happened before?" he asked.

"Not like that." I looked down at the river.

"Perri, tell us," Mama said, tapping her foot.

"Okay," I said, looking away. I hadn't connected this last episode with the previous ones.

"A couple weeks ago, I was going down to the river, and, um, not paying attention, and almost stepped into that hole by the big tree, only I just floated over it. I'd forgot about it by the time I got home."

"I thought someone was supposed to fill that in," Mama said, looking at Uncle Adam.

"I'll tell Emek. He was to get someone to do it. Was that the only time?"

"Well, there was when Peter and I were up looking for mushrooms." I saw Peter shaking his head. "He climbed a tree, a branch broke and somehow he fell sideways into a mossbush instead of on the ground." I also ignored his glare.

"I see," Uncle Adam said.

"We'll have to get with Bay and see what we can do about it," Mama said. "You have no warning of these episodes?"

"No. It just happens." I scuffed my bare toe in the dirt.

"Think about it, about anything you may have felt or sensed just before it happened," Mama said. "Are you going to eat with us, or with Bay and Pauli?"

"With you." I was still shaken and wanted to be at home, even though Charley would be at his folks' home.

"Come along, then."

"Bye, Uncle Adam," Peter and I said in unison.

He went off toward the meeting center, and Peter and I followed Mama up the hill. I had a feeling things were going to get worse. I had no idea how much worse.

Chapter 2   High Council

Mama and I glanced out at the forest as we chopped vegetables by the kitchen window.

"I remember another forest, on another world far away," Mama said. I knew she was trying to keep my mind off my problem Talent, but I'd always loved to listen to her stories of other worlds.

"We were at a cabin, saying farewell to my mother and Uncle Pete, Larry's father. They were twins."

"I know." Larry was Papa.

"I've often wished I could ask Mom about raising girls," Mama continued. "But that's so long ago and far away, and I never did regain my memories of growing up there. Just bits and pieces. Larry grew up with my sister and me, you know. His mom died shortly after he was born."

I nodded. "How could you leave your family?" I couldn't imagine being without mine, even if I only had Peter.

Mama looked at the knife in her hand. "They were a lot older when we went back to Earth. Bill, whom my sister, Beth, was pregnant with when we left, was grown up, and she'd had five more. Pauli and Allen and the three who stayed there. Mom and Uncle Pete were old. It wasn't the same, especially without my memories. But I still miss them. And Aunt Dalia and her family. She was Dad's long lost sister, and Bay's grandmother." Uncle Bay was Charley's papa and Aunt Pauli was his mama.

I blinked. How did that work out? We had a family tree written out, but the fact that Mama and Papa were twenty years younger than they should have been always confused me. Papa said that was because of all their space travels.

My knife slipped, but stopped just short of my finger. "Did you see that?"

"Yes dear. Pay attention to what you're doing."

#

After supper, the head council met at our cabin. Mama, Papa, Uncle Adam, Uncle Bay, Aunt Pauli, and Emek comprised the group, and I was allowed to listen in but not comment. Emek, blond, with a round face and very widely spaced eyes, like all the Bramites, took his position seriously. He was a direct descendent of their prophet, Bram.

Uncle Adam announced the three topics; tree bugs, low river, and a second settlement. Emek had talked with the head treecutter, Dirl, and he would bring in some infected branches for the scientific guys to look at.

"Since we didn't get our normal winter rain," Uncle Adam said, "the river is much lower than normal for this time of year. There is barely enough to keep the mill running. We will have to set stricter rules on water use."

"Does the river up north have enough volume to run a mill?" Papa drawled, crossing his legs.

"That's one of the things we need to find out," Uncle Adam said. "Bay and Bill will handle the bug problem, along with Art and his scientific people. Now for the new settlement."

"No," Mama said, sitting up. "Two days is just too far away. Right, Bay?"

Uncle Bay nodded.

"There's nothing closer with an adequate water supply," Papa said. "Art is working on a desalinization plant to use seawater, but it could be awhile, if ever, before he comes up with a working model. We can't count on that." The science guys used a lot of stuff from the spaceship, still in orbit, but couldn't always find what they wanted. The Wati had a shuttle and let us use it when we needed to go up to the ship. She had been pretty much stripped by now.

"If we did not have our Fours, I would agree with you, Lyn," Uncle Adam said. "But with them, we can always stay in contact."

I saw Emek wince. He hated not having our mindlink, even though he couldn't know the depth of our Talents. The Fours were links between four of us that created an entity stronger than the four separately. First Four was Mama, Uncle Adam, Uncle Bay, and Aunt Pauli. Second Four was Gabe, Uncle Adam's eldest son; Charley, and Peter and me.

Emek also hated having to share the overseeing of the colony with Uncle Adam and Papa. Even though we couldn't mindlink with the Bramites, I could *sense* their emotions.

"Larry, how do you feel about a new settlement," Uncle Adam asked.

"I'd like to see what we can do here first," he drawled. "I don't care for splitting us up."

"Perri?"

"I think we ought to at least start looking for a place. It's going to get very crowded after the next bonding and a new crop of babies."

"That's my point," Uncle Adam said. "I propose we send Allen with a small team up to the north river to gather information on it and the area. Information is always useful. Any objections?"

Mama wore a stubborn expression, but agreed, as did Papa and Uncle Bay.

"For information only," Mama said.

"Good. I will send Gabriel, he will be our contact. Anything else?"

"Yes," Mama said, chewing her knuckle. 'Perri's Talent has developed a new twist you should all know about. Basically, she can levitate people when they are in harm's way, but as of yet has no control over it. People need to understand this and not take it out on her. She's still a child herself."

I shook my head.

"She's a grown woman and betrothed to my son, and she needs to learn how to control it," Uncle Bay said. To Emek, he added, "Has a time been set for next bonding?"

"It will be twenty-three days from now," Emek said. "I believe most have made their selections."

"Good," Uncle Adam said. "Anything else? Okay, meeting adjourned." He and Emek left.

Mama walked out with Uncle Bay. "Keep Perri away from the others as much as possible," he said. "Charley is building them a house up here by ours. Have her work with him. I don't want this to happen again."

He should know by now Mama would send *me whatever he said about me.*

"What about her class and other work down below?"

"We'll take care of that later."

Oh yeah, I thought.

Chapter 3   North Point

Two days passed without any further outbreak of freaky Talent. Mama had switched my duty schedule so that most of the time I was working on my house. It was hard to imagine living somewhere other than Mama's.

Sometimes I thought of my childhood days, when life was so much simpler, and my main focus was on getting away from Peter. I knew he had to stay near me when we weren't at home, he was my ears. I *heard* whatever he heard. Still, I wanted to be by myself sometimes.

#

One morning, a few days later, Charley and I met with several others to see Uncle Allen, Gabriel, and their group off on their trek up to the north river. Uncle Allen had been up there a long time ago and said it should be possible.

I wished we could go with them, but Mama had made it very clear we were to stay here. I knew she was of mixed minds. Strongly against splitting up the colony, she was also aware that we needed to know what was up there. I kept my desire to go, to be away from her, hidden in my secret place in my mind, as we returned to our duties.

After the reading class I taught, I went by the craft area where Mama was teaching younger women how to sew. Several of their mothers were there, demanding that Mama stop this nonsense about a northern settlement.

"We know our children will want to go, but they can't be allowed to take our grandchildren away from us," Treesa said. She and her mate, Barad, had accompanied Mama and Papa through the tunnels on Brama. Since the Bramites had left their cavern home, where they'd been limited to two children, grandchildren had become much more abundant.

"I've been telling them, but I can't stop it by myself," Mama said. "We need to organize a group of you to go before the council, with a list of all the reasons not to go up there."

"When will there be another meeting?"

"Most likely when the explorers return. I'll let you know, Treesa."

"Is well. Come, friends." She led the other mothers away.

"You see how it is?" Mama looked at me. "We can cut down one more row of trees to squeeze in more houses, according to Karil. That'll do for another two or three years."

"That's just pushing it off," I said, sitting beside her. A couple of the girls nodded. "We'll still have to do it eventually. Or else stop having babies."

"Never," said one of the girls.

"When we have another generation of adults. How's your sewing?"

I escaped a little later, grabbed a bite at the provisions center, and ran into Anne and Joan, Art and Betty's eldest daughter.

"We're going to meet Beth. Come on," Joan said.

"What's up?" The four of us, close in age, were cousins and best friends. We ran down to the overlook where Beth, Charley's sister, waited. I sensed a secret. It was the one place no one, like brothers, could sneak up on us and eavesdrop.

As soon as I saw Beth, pink with excitement, I knew. She and Gabe had been bonded the year before and had not been able to conceive.

"Guess what? I think I'm pregnant," she blurted as we gathered around. We all shrieked.

I focused on her. "You are," I said. The others stared at me. "I can *sense* it. Have you told Gabe or your mama?" All of a sudden I felt uncomfortable with these girls I'd known all my life, and with the idea I could tell what was going on in other people's bodies.

"I think Mama knows, and I'm waiting for Gabe to get back so I can tell him in person."

I took a deep breath. Part of my Talent duty was to help bring it out in others, but I'd never done anything like this. "Look inside you," I told Beth. "Close your eyes, and you two," I looked at Anne and Joan, "be very quiet. You should be able to do it, Beth. You and Charley are beyond your folks."

I watched as Beth closed her eyes, and *went in* with her, not *touching*, not letting her know I was there. The other two held their breaths.

Beth gasped and shrieked when she found the tiny newness. I twitched out.

"Oh, Perri, you knew." Beth hugged me. The others hugged Beth.

"I went in and counted my eggs once," I said. "I'll have to have a lot of twins."

"Next year you'll be looking at your own," Beth said, still dancing up and down.

"We all will," Joan said.

Except me," Anne added. She was the youngest. "I have to wait another year for Peter and me to be bonded. But I feel ready now, and I know Peter is."

I nodded. My twin had no secrets from me.

"Let's go down to the beach," Beth said.

"Our duties," Joan pointed out.

"Oh, come on." Anne followed Beth toward the beach downstream from the overlook.

#

When I got home, Mama and Charley stood with arms crossed on the porch. "Where have you been?" Mama demanded, frowning, as if she didn't know. I *sent* to her that Beth was pregnant.

"We went down to the beach to celebrate."

"That's what Beth said." Charley unwound his arms and stepped toward me. "You two, Anne and Joan."

"Well, none of us had anything really important to do."

"Some people didn't think so," Mama said, dropping her arms.

"We run this place smoothly because everyone does what they're supposed to do when they're supposed to do it," Charley said. He took my arm and led me down the steps. "When you become my mate, I expect you to behave responsibly."

I yanked away from him, my mood plummeting. He was going to be as bad as Mama. "Well, we're not bonded yet, so until then I'll just do what I want." I stomped down the trail, around the first curve, stopped and fumed. This growing up stuff was no fun at all.

When I calmed down and went back, he was gone. All Mama said was, "You'll understand when you have children."

Chapter 4   The First Gate

Peter and I waited over on the sea beach for the explorers to return. Gabe had *let us know* they were coming. Breezes off the sea tousled our curls as the sun lowered itself into the watery horizon.

I thought of when the families had come over here when we were kids. Mama called it a holiday. Peter and I had chased each other up and down the beach, in and out of the water. It had been a long time since we'd wrestled in the sand.

"There they are," Peter said, pointing. We rushed along the beach to meet them.

"What is it like?" I demanded.

Uncle Allen grinned. "Looks good."

"After the council meets, we'll make an announcement," Gabe added. "How'd they let you two out?"

"Mama said we could come because otherwise we'd drive her crazy," Peter said.

"That figures." Uncle Allen drew us along with the group. We hiked over the low dunes and across to the main trail up to the settlement. Back at the plaza, a mob of young people bombarded us with questions.

"After the council meeting, we'll have answers," Uncle Allen said after he called for silence. "Don't even think of going up there yet."

I knew there were some who'd sneak off in the night anyway, but no big loss. Uncle Allen reported that the site looked good, the river appeared adequate for a small settlement, and there was no sign of the tree bugs.

"We can keep it in mind for later," Mama said.

At the council meeting, Uncle Allen reported in a little more detail, and Treesa presented her friends' concerns. The council agreed to shelve the North River project for this year. It was time to prepare the fields for the summer crops.

The young people continued to talk about it. Several young couples still lived in their parents' houses because they could not find a suitable place to build their own. I just wanted to go up and see the place.

#

One morning, Charley caught me on the way down the hill. "Uncle Adam's mate, Aunt Kareth, talked him and Emek into doing a group trek up north," he said. "Do you wanna go?"

"Of course, but I thought they didn't want to do anything about it for a while."

"More and more people younger than our folks want to go up, and they're putting pressure on the council. Dad wants to go and see for himself."

"Okay. When?" I did a little hop.

"Two days. They have to rearrange duty schedules." I couldn't wait, but knew I had to.

That evening, when Mama had gone over to see Aunt Pauli, and I was cleaning up the dishes, Peter said, "Did you know Mama and Aunt Pauli are going with us?"

"Aunt Pauli, yes. But Mama? She can't. I'm going with Charley, I don't need her." I smashed a cup against the wall.

He took another cup away from me and said, "She's not going just to keep an eye on us. She has to go because she's on the head council."

"Why didn't she tell me? She even hid it in her mind." I stomped around the room.

"Maybe because she didn't want to get in a shouting match with you." Peter twiddled a hair on his chin.

"What about a shouting match?" Mama said, in the doorway.

"Um, I told her you were going," Peter said, ducking his head. I looked at him and realized that he'd hidden it too.

"Peter," I began.

"Hush," Mama said. "Yes I'm going, because I want to see for myself, too. Does something about that bother you?"

"No. I just wondered why you didn't tell me." I knew it was more than that, but kept my mouth shut.

#

The two days of preparation passed like a snail climbing up a tree. I swear the sun stopped in in the sky.

When we finally left on the third morning, I made sure that Charley and I were at the front. Peter ran back and forth. Mama walked farther back, with the older folk. We each carried a backpack with supplies for six days. The day was warm and sunny, with more trees popping out new leaves and tiny flowers.

We took the cutoff over to the sea beach and walked along the hard sand. Here, just north of the river's mouth, the tan beach sprawled wide, but presently it narrowed. The forest came down to the edge of the sand in many places, and there were times we had to walk under the trees.

I drank in the sea smell and the dancing breezes. In the afternoon, the sea breeze stiffened and cooled us from the hot sun. As it lowered, we began looking for a place to camp. Uneasiness crept over me, but I couldn't figure out why. There was no danger I could *sense.*

"This looks good," Uncle Bay said. We'd come to a place where a couple of big trees had fallen and left an open space. A stream meandered down nearby. The men starting building a fire pit.

The uneasiness grew. We'd never found any sign of large beasts, only the little creatures of the forest and sea, and the chickens we'd brought. Papa said Harmony was not in a natural stage of evolution.

As I pulled out what I needed from my pack, I looked at the sea and saw the rock. It was high and wide, a few house widths offshore. Something on its flat top shimmered against the sky and drew me to it.

I dropped my bread and walked down the beach, into the sea. Halfway out to the rock, Charley and Peter grabbed my arms and carried me back to the beach.

"Hey," I yelped, shaking my head to clear it.

"What the hell were you doing?" Charley demanded, dropping me on the sand and plopping down beside me.

"There's something out there I have to see." I struggled against him, but he held me tight and called the first Four. Together they neutralized the pull the thing had on me. Charley let me go, but didn't leave my side.

I sat back, rubbing my shoulder. "I've never felt anything like that before, and don't want to again. It felt like it was trying to pull my Talent out of me."

"I wish I knew more about your Talent," Charley said, gently pulling me back to him. "You've got things in you none of us can figure out."

"Including me." I sagged against him.

Mama came over. "Are you all right?" she asked, touching my shoulder. I nodded. "Then let's get supper going." Charley helped me up and I followed her to the cook site.

I noticed Mama keeping an eye on me, and Charley was never far away. When I took a pot of vegetables over to the camp table, Peter followed me.

"Go bother someone else," I said. He grinned and sat down. After supper, the group talked about the new place, and sang some songs. Charley took me aside for some smooching.

As we prepared for bed, I glanced out at the rock. It still glowed. Mama had me sleep between Aunt Pauli and her, up under the trees. Twice in the hours before dawn, I tried to get up, and twice they held me down.

In the morning, I snuck away, on excuse of needing to squat behind a bush, and sat and looked at the rock. There was only a faint pull from here. I *reached*. There was something, a tear in reality, but no sense of danger. I'd have to go out there some time, there might be a threat to the community. But not today.

"Any danger to us?" Mama asked, sitting beside me. She knew me too well.

"I don't sense any."

"Well then, let's not worry about it, but keep an eye on that thing. If you sense a change, let me know."

"Yes, Mama."

#

We reached the north river shortly before sundown and found the campsite of the previous group. Dumping our packs, we set up our camp, and prepared our evening meal. As we were relaxing after supper, I thought of the big rock in the sea where we camped the previous night. It had drawn me to it, as if it had wanted something from me. But what? I'd *sensed* no danger from the rock itself, but something about it made me uneasy.

"Hey, Perri, we're singing the travel song." Peter poked me in the ribs. I joined in.

In the morning, we wandered around, looking at everything. The cliffs on the north side were higher than those at River Point, and there wasn't as much open space along the river.

When someone mentioned the latter, Gabe said the flat area went much farther upriver than that at River Point.

The hills were lower up here, and the trees farther apart. Charley and I found a place on a hill overlooking the river and the sea that we marked for our someday house.

Papa and Emek marked out places for the mill and the gathering house. The men built one small house, to see how it weathered. And still I felt Mama's unease. I wanted to shout, "We'll be fine up here," but I kept it to myself.

Charley and Peter and I wandered up into the hills looking for fruit trees. We found some that looked like our nut trees, but there were no nuts on them. Up higher, we found a small grove of trees with white blossoms, unlike anything we'd ever seen.

"This looks like some kind of fruit tree," Charley said, plucking a twig with several flowers. "I'll take this back and see if anyone has any ideas about it."

Back at camp, he showed the twig around.

Papa took it and sniffed the blossoms. "Apples," he said with a grin.

Mama took it and smelled them. "Nice." She handed them to me. "Perri, can you tell anything?"

I touched a leaf. "I don't *sense* any danger or wrongness. When is the fruit ripe?"

"In the fall. We'll definitely have to come up then."

"Will they grow down at River Point?" Mama asked.

"I don't know. They need cool weather. Let's not tell the others just yet. I want to be sure the fruit is edible."

After an evening of discussion, we decided that this place was a good possibility when we wanted to expand.

"But not yet," Mama said. "Pack up, we leave in the morning."

#

On the way back we camped by the rock again. After dark, I saw a shimmery light above it.

"Do you see that, Charley?" I asked, pointing.

"What?"

I explained, but he couldn't see it. I found Mama and pointed to the rock. "Look."

"I see a faint light on it, is that what you mean?"

"It's bright and full of colors. Mama, I have to go and look." I didn't know how long it would be before I would get up this way again.

"No." Mama grabbed my arm. "You're not going anywhere near that thing."

"I have to." The pull of the shimmer grew stronger, and yanked me away from Mama's grip. As I found myself running out into the sea, I *heard* Mama calling for Charley. I fought it, but I could not stop.

Chapter 5   Visions

I ran up crudely cut steps in the rock to the top. Layers of lavender fog shimmered in front of me. As I stretched my hands into it, I felt Charley's strong arms around my waist. Soft goo surrounded my hands, and I yanked them back. Charley took a step back, then forward to regain his balance. My head jerked forward, into the goo.

Someone was holding my legs, pulling on them. My head was in a fantastical, mysterious space. Swirling greenness, a minty spicy sort of smell, a sense of something else my brain could not process surrounded me. The men pulled me out and Charley carried me back to the beach.

"Are you all right?" he asked, sitting down with me as Mama rushed up.

"What did you see?" Peter sat in front of me, others clustering around.

I leaned against Charley, still shaking. Mama took my hand.

I gathered my breath and said, "A whole 'nother world. Greenish, and a strange smell."

"I don't *see* any damage," Mama said, *probing* me. I agreed, but something had dug into my mind for a moment. I would have to check it out later, when I was alone.

"I'm okay now. It won't bother me any more today." I paused and looked around at the people I knew so well. "It's a Gate. A doorway to other worlds. And way too close to our community."

"Perhaps we should look southward," someone said.

"Too hot and swampy," Papa replied. "No other rivers."

"We need to stay in this area," Gabe said. "My mother's people, the older ones, will not move again. They'll stay at River Point. Let's turn in and get an early start in the morning."

When everyone had settled down for the night, I allowed myself to dig out and open the memory of the Gate. There was the force, trying to pull me through, a force no one else had felt, stronger than Charley's Talent, a force with awareness.

It had picked around in my brain, and yes, there had been something added. Cautiously I *touched* it. *Information. About what?* I shivered and huddled in my blanket.

The sea continued its eternal lapping. Something whispered in the forest. Sea smell and woodsy aroma mingled in my nose. A cool breeze circled about.

Did I dare access it? I debated for a while, and decided to sleep on it. Later, when the stars had turned halfway across the sky and I was still awake, I decided to go ahead.

The information was a series of pictures of places. There were green valleys, beaches with great waves of water splashing on them, golden plains, piles of rocks, a place where water lay under ragged trees, great groups of glistening spires. And a smooth white beach with turquoise sea, trees with long fronds, bushes with huge red flowers. I managed to hold onto that one, as the rest faded away.

Was this a list of places that one could go to through the Gate? I sat up. That beach. Would just keeping that picture in my mind get me there? I tucked it away in a secret corner of my mind. And then I thought, would I be able to get back? I wanted to try it, but didn't dare. I'd have to have someone go with me. Peter? It would be a secret thing to think about when I needed a cheer up.

Chapter 6   Perri and Charley

Back at River Point we were met by a group of young people, led by Beth and Joan. "How was it?" Beth asked. "When can we move up?"

"Don't even think about that," Mama said.

"The place has future possibilities," Uncle Adam added. "The full council will meet tomorrow night and after that we will make an announcement. Now return to your tasks."

"Or your suppers," Mama added. Beth and Joan accompanied us up to our house. Charley went with his folks. Mama and I collapsed while the girls fixed our supper. Papa stretched out his legs and leaned back in his big chair. He and Mama weren't used to that kind of hike.

In the morning, I returned to my duties, but Mama took a day off. When I returned for dinner and went into my room, I *sensed* Mama and Papa talking as they entered the house after me.

"I'm sure she's hiding something from me," Mama said.

"How? I thought the kids' minds were open books to you."

I shivered. They were talking about me. I knew I should go out and let them know I was here, but I was curious to *hear* what they were going to say.

"She's learned to hide some things from me and the others." I could picture Mama chewing on her knuckle.

"Sixteen-year-old girls always have secrets from their moms," Papa said.

"How do you know?" *Just what I wanted to ask.*

"You were sixteen once, even if you don't remember it."

"I know," Mama said.

I wondered what it was like not knowing what you did when you were a child. I could remember most everything. Like the time when I ran into the woods to get away from Peter and I couldn't find my way out. Mama had a fit, and when they found me, she punished Peter for not staying with me.

"You had a crush on an undesirable boy," Papa continued. "Mom forbade you to see him, you snuck out one night to meet him, and I followed you. I was sleeping on the screen porch then, and you woke me up going through."

Mama made a mumbly sort of sound.

"You got in his car and I followed you in mine. At Palm, you jumped out of his car and started running home. Fortunately, there wasn't much traffic, so I could go slow and keep an eye on you. I'm sure you never told Mom, because you never said anything to me."

"Oh," Mama said, with that funny tone in her voice whenever she said something to do with her lost memories. "And you never told me." So Mama had done naughty things, too, when she was young. I tried not to feel too smug.

"I figured it'd just make things worse," Papa said. "You sulked for days."

"Oh. Well, thanks, I guess," she said. There was a pause long enough for a kiss. "But there's still the problem of Perri." I rolled my eyes. "She's learning things I can't even imagine doing."

"She can take care of herself."

"Would you say that if she were yours?"

I gasped. I'd never have believed Mama would say that to his face. I'd known that Uncle Adam was our biological father ever since I was five. Papa knocked his chair back and tore out of the house.

Mama would probably have given anything except Peter and me to have those words back. She didn't say anything, but slammed into her room. I tiptoed out and came back in the front door.

"Anyone here?" I called.

After a moment, Mama stalked out of her room and stared at me. "Did you just get here?" I nodded, blanking my mind. "You heard us didn't you?"

I could only nod. I'd never been able to lie to her.

"Keep it to yourself." She turned and strode into her room.

"Okay," I called after her. "He'll be back." I wished I'd never heard it as I went to get something to eat.

#

That evening I chose to eat with Charley and his family. I couldn't face my folks. Sometimes I hated my Talent. It was too easy to hear something I wish I hadn't.

Uncle Bay, tall and thin, had brown curls and a narrow face; and Aunt Pauli looked like a younger Mama. In addition to Charley's sister Beth, who took after their father, he had two younger sisters, Megan and Mandy, and a young brother, Bobby

"So how's the house coming?" Uncle Bay asked Charley.

"It's not. The builders are all working on other houses, and I haven't had time to work on it myself." Charley pushed his potatoes around his plate.

"You can't stay here after you're bonded," Aunt Pauli said. "I promised Bobby your room."

"Mom."

"You know the rules, son," Uncle Bay said.

"Yes, Dad. But how can I work on our house when I have to work in the fields?"

"I'll get Adam to authorize a half day each."

'I thought we were going to live up north,' I *sent* to Charley on our private link.

'Next year,' he replied the same way.

After supper, Charley walked me down to the council meeting. He talked about our house, how we were going to live, and raise our children. I mostly tuned him out. I didn't want to think about that yet.

Hours of debate later, the council decided to approve the site, but not do anything with it until next spring. I was disappointed, but not terribly so.

Charley and I lagged behind the others going up to our homes. "If we're going to follow the tradition, we shouldn't wait any longer," he said, arm around my waist. Bramite tradition, adopted since the exodus from the cavern, praised young women who had a baby on the way at bonding. Our generation had chosen to follow it.

I squeezed him. "Mama wants me to wait until we're bonded."

"Your mama grew up on another world, and you're not your mama's little girl any more. You are a grown up woman and my partner in life. You have to decide, not her."

I sighed. He still didn't understand how connected a mother and daughter with Talent were. It was far more complicated than with him and his folks. "I know," I said, "but I'm scared."

"That's normal. I'll be gentle." He stopped and pulled me into a hug. "I do love you."

"Me too," I said, kissing him.

We continued on and I looked within myself. I knew I must have a daughter in the next few years, to continue the family, and to move forward in the quest to bring Mama's Earth into the Consortium, whatever that was. But that was way in my daughter's daughter's future. Meanwhile, my body was ready.

"Where and when?"

"Tomorrow night. Up in the glade. Okay?" He stopped, pulled me around, and kissed me wildly. "I've waited so long," he said into my hair.

"You had to wait awhile for me, didn't you?" I murmured into his chest. He was almost four years older and had let go of his childhood long ago. I was still clinging to mine.

"I thought you'd never grow up." He let me go. When we reached my folks' cabin, he kissed me briefly and strode off. In the house, Mama gave me a little half smile as I ran into my room. She knew.

I tingled with anticipation, trembled with fear, and could not sleep. I knew all about it, pain and bleeding and ecstasy, and that one of my defenses would be broken. He came to me in my dreams, but I woke before it ended.

The next day I stumbled through my tasks, and ate with Charley's family again. "Be sure to leave time for your supper to digest," Uncle Bay said with a twinkle in his eye. Aunt Pauli giggled. I *knew* she was thinking of her first time with him.

When we were finally allowed to leave, we ran up to the glade. Charley grabbed me, swung me around, kissed me soundly, and set me down. "I love you so."

"Me, too," I said. "Are we going to do it on the ground?" I hugged myself and pulled at a curl. All the anxiety and excitement came tumbling back.

"No." He fetched a roll of blankets he'd hidden up here earlier, and piled them on the ground. "Our first bed."

He pulled me down onto the blankets and we sat together, suddenly shy. I leaned into him and he put an arm around me. I could *feel* his desire in my mind and teased at it. He kicked off his sandals and removed his tunic. I undid my sandals and lifted off my tunic.

My body wanted it, but my self was not ready. I liked Charley a lot, and was ready to spend the rest of my life with him, but I was in love with Gabe and had always dreamed of giving myself to him first.

Charley pulled me down on the blankets, dropped his trousers, knelt beside me, spread my legs. As he kissed me here and there, my mind went blank as I shoved my self into a cupboard in my mind, and my body welcomed him in.

Later, lying quietly in his arms, I sensed a completeness that had not been there before. Inwardly, I steered the sperm to my egg. I wondered what it was like for the Bramite women, and Betty, who didn't know whether they had conceived until many days later.

I awoke at first light, kissed him, and slipped away, back to my folks' house. Mama came out of her room as I entered the front door.

"It went well," she said.

"Yes, Mama. Now I wish I hadn't waited so long."

"They always say that. Will you conceive?"

"I'm planning on it." Except I had no idea what pregnancy and taking care of a new baby would be like.

Mama hugged me and wept a few tears into my hair. "It's your turn now."

Chapter 7   Cray

I helped Charley work on our little house, along with my regular duties. It kept me busy and from dwelling on the future. Although the Gate remained in my thoughts, I didn't talk about it. Someday I would figure out how to go through it, but what concerned me more was what could come through it into our world.

#

Two days later, Peter and I got leave to hike up into the hills to look for early fruits and nuts. It had been awhile since we'd been able to get away, and we needed the time alone together. Even when we tried to block them out, the others were still always there in our minds.

The trees were mostly leaved out and full of chatterers, little brown critters that reminded Papa of squirrels. We breathed in the natural, wild air and relaxed.

As we trotted up the trail along the river, I felt my whole being. I sensed all living things; Peter saw how everything worked together. I let him lead, he was faster now, with his long legs. A narrow trail had been here when Mama and all had first arrived.

We found the manyan fruits beginning to ripen and a few were ready to pick. The nuts were still green, and we stopped to rest at a little overlook from where we could see the river, cropland beyond it, and distantly to the right, the sea.

"You never told me what you saw at the Gate," Peter said.

"I don't want to talk about it, but here, you can look." I opened that particular memory to him.

"Wow. I wonder how that works."

"I don't care how it works, but I have to go through and find out what's there, if there's a way to keep whatever from coming through. I'm responsible for the safety of the community now, Mama and me."

"We all are."

"You and I. We're the chosen ones." I twisted a curl. I couldn't find the words I wanted. "And I'm afraid I can't do it."

Peter *sent* me a soothing touch and said, "Sure you can, sis." He made patterns in the dirt with a finger. "You've got me and the Fours."

"I keep thinking of more and more bad things that could happen to us, and what, if anything, I could do about them." I hugged myself.

"You need to think the other way around," Peter said. "Look at all the good stuff, how well things are going here, how we have everything we really need. You're going to be bonded with Charley, and there's the feast after, and all those fun things. And everyone's strong and healthy."

"Except Aunt Alice," I said. Elderly and frail, Aunt Alice, Doc Richard's wife, was the oldest person in the colony. Doc was the eldest of Mama's cousins.

"Well, she's really old. So why worry about something that doesn't exist."

"Because it might, and we need to be prepared." I jumped up. "I'm going up to check the berries. Coming?"

"No, I need to think about something. I'll be with you."

I continued up the trail, knowing I could *reach* Peter any time. Although I couldn't hear what was going on around me, I felt safe. I thought about the pictures of places in my mind, and that led to Harmony. It had been an empty world when Judee, the Wati, had found it, so why would anyone have a Gate here? I thought of Uncle Bill and Uncle Bay talking about the lack of large animals here. *Would someone put some through someday?*

"No," I said aloud. Stopping in a small glade, I could glimpse the river through the trees. They would not, could not, take our world. We would stay here no matter what. I *searched* for danger and found none. But there was something large and alive up ahead. Immediately shutting down my Talent, except for a hair-thin link to Peter, I crept up the trail, eyes wide open.

Finally I pinpointed it, *reached* for an instant, and backed off. It was sentient! Chills rippled my spine. I wanted to turn back to Peter, but I had to find out more about it. Humanoid, it crouched behind bushes, anxious, uncomfortable, annoyed at the one who had sent it here, and underneath, pleasure at being here.

I drew back down the trail and waited. So someone had sent it? Why?

'To spy out the land.'

'Peter!' I was just able to keep from saying it aloud. Who knew what kind of hearing the alien had. It did not move, so I tiptoed up the trail until I'd almost reached the bush it hid behind. Now I could feel the alien's pain, which it was trying to hide.

I *touched* it briefly, sensed a call for help. Our first rule was that anything unusual was to be immediately reported to one of the first Four, but I was up here and they were down there. There was no danger, and it needed help. I pushed through between bushes and knelt down by its side. No, it was male. His side.

"Sorry," I said. "Where are you hurt?"

We stared at each other. He had a long, very narrow face, small eyes above flat nose and round mouth. I assumed he had ears under the dark brown hair that hung to his eyes and shoulders. A strange, sweetish smell tickled my nose. He said something which I couldn't hear, and I put my hands over my ears.

He pulled out a little device, looked at it, touched something on it, and put it away. I *felt* his mind. His name was Cray, he'd come through a Gate in the mountains several days back, sent by others to check this world, and leave by the Gate on the rock.

As I tried to assimilate this, I noticed his foot sticking out to the side, and realized that was where the pain was coming from. I touched it gently. He winced, but didn't move it. Closing my eyes, I *probed* and found tearing and twisting. With my most delicate touch, I *untwisted* and *reconnected*, then withdrew. I found some vines to bind his foot over the brown cloth boot with a hard sole.

To get his mind off his pain, I *showed* him Peter, part of our community, crop fields. Finally he nodded and knelt on the injured leg. I helped him up. He was as tall as Charley, but not nearly as wide. As I handed him his bundle, I saw that he had six fingers on each hand. His walking stick was of a dark wood I'd never seen, with carvings of strange things.

Out on the trail, Cray *sent* a thankful feeling, and limped into the forest on the west side. He shooed me back when I tried to follow.

I watched him disappear into the trees. Not a normally fearful person, I still wondered at my lack of apprehension. Maybe somewhere underneath I'd expected him, or someone, to come. I hoped it hadn't been because I'd accidently put my head through the Gate.

Would Cray be all right? Would he make it to the Gate? Would he tell whoever sent him about me, our community? Would they come through, or send someone else? Would they try to harm us? All I had were questions.

At least Cray was much like us, so probably the others were too. He had courage to come to a new world. Of course, he might not have had a choice. They could have just given him the bundle and shoved him through, but how would that get them whatever they wanted to know about Harmony?

I did know I'd like to get to know him better.

'Hey, Perri,' Peter *sent*, coming up behind me. 'What was it?'

I turned to look at him. "An offworlder. Come on." I led the way up the trail, and found footprints. Very long and narrow. They continued, facing us, up along the river after the trail curled west, up to the rocky place where the river curved.

"So it came out of the mountains," Pete said. "I wonder if there's another Gate up there."

"He said there is, several days back. Now we've got to watch the mountains, too." I tugged at a curl. "We'll need to send an expedition up to find it."

"Yeah, but what was it?" Peter turned and started back down.

"Like a man, very thin. He had some sort of mind link."

"Hadn't we better let the rest of the Fours know?"

"Yes. When we get back to where he was." We walked silently, each deep in our own thoughts.

At the bushes I stopped at the place where Cray had hidden. We joined, and *reached* for Gabe and Charley. They brought in the first Four, and I showed them what I had experienced.

'Oh my Oneness,' Mama *said*.

'Come home now,' Uncle Bay *added*. 'We'll meet at Lyn's.'

Chapter 8   Judee and her Girls

"So we're not safe here anymore," Mama said. The rest of the Fours and Papa had gathered at our cabin. She looked at me. "Why did you let it see you?"

"He was hurting," I said, collapsing on the couch. "I had to help him. There was no danger."

"These people who sent him could be very dangerous." Uncle Adam glared at me. "Are you sure he was the only one?"

"Yes. There was only one set of footprints."

"But more could come through at any time," Uncle Bay said. "We need a full time watch up there." He looked around. "Peter, find out from Art if he's got anything we can use as a warning signal. We'll have to set up something for the one at the rock, too."

I had a feeling he'd half expected this to happen.

"Like a motion sensor?" Peter asked.

"That would be a start," Larry drawled. "But what about things that don't register on it? Or things that fly? You'd have to put something up in the trees for that."

"I'll talk to Uncle Art about it," Peter said. "He'll figure something out."

"That may let us know they're coming, but we also need a way to stop them," Uncle Adam pointed out.

"We could build a trap for one like Perri saw," Uncle Bay said, "but that wouldn't work if a lot of them came through, and we don't know anything about them, like what they can do and what tools they might have."

"So we have to defend ourselves against a total unknown," Mama muttered.

"I could go through the Gate and find out about them," I said.

"Absolutely not," Mama said, standing up in front of me. She added, "Don't you even think about it, Miss Perri."

"Yes, Mama." I paused and twiddled a curl. "But I got the impression that the main difference between the ones who sent Cray, and Cray's people is that the others are a lot smarter."

"Wonderful," Charley said. "I wish you'd left it alone."

"You'd rather have us not know anything about another Gate and that someone could come through it to spy on us or hurt us?" I asked.

"We need every bit of information we can get," Gabe said.

"Yes, I agree," Uncle Adam added. "Now, the people need to be told at least enough so they know what is going on. We can't guarantee it'll be one of us who sees them first next time. I'll tell Emek."

"Let's start with the kids. They're always more open to new things," Mama said. "Perri and Pauli and I will sit down and figure out how and what to tell them so they'll understand the danger, but not be scared silly."

"A lot of Bramites won't believe us," I said.

"The kids will, dear. That's why we go to them first. Adam, just send out a notice that the twins saw something unusual at the top of the trail and if anyone else sees anything to let us know."

"They'll want to know what it was," Aunt Pauli said.

"Tell them that's all we know right now."

"Good," Uncle Bay said. "I'll get with Allen to set up an exploration team. How far do you think it is to this gate in the mountains?"

"He said several days back, so I'd say four or five at least. Look for long, narrow footprints," I said.

"Right. You kids stay in town. There may be others out there."

"I'll see that she does," Charley said. I felt the link between father and son.

"You don't own me yet," I said, standing up.

"Bonding is not owning."

"All right, you two," Mama said, on her feet. "I need to get back to my duties, and I'm sure you do too. See you later." The group broke up and Charley took me off to the glade.

"We need to talk," he said.

"Now what?"

"We're going to be bonded in a few days. I want you with me, not your mama."

"Now wait a minute. I have to work with her all the time, whether you and I are bonded or not." I snatched a leaf off a tree. "She'll always be my mama and I'm not going to stop seeing her."

"I'm just saying if you have a problem, come to me first."

"Even if it's a woman or baby problem?" I stepped toward him and he stepped back.

"Uh, well, tell me first, then you can talk to your mama about it." He scuffed the leaves with the toes of his sandal. "I mean, we're a pair now, we have to do things together, with each other. You can't be running off all the time with Peter, either. I don't hang around with my brother and sisters all the time."

"Your brother is ten years younger than you, of course you don't. Peter's my twin, that's more than just a brother. We have a special bond between us, from before we were born." I stared at him. "Who appointed you my boss?"

"I'm not." He took another step back. "I just want you to be aware of things you're doing now that are not appropriate for a bonded woman."

"What difference does it make? I know I'll be living in your house instead of my folks', and running it, and having your children, but I don't see why I can't spend time with Mama and Peter and anyone else I want to."

"Once the children start coming, you won't have time. Ask my mama."

In his face again, I said, "Don't you think Mama hasn't taught me everything I need to know to run a household? Don't you think she hasn't taught me how to behave as a bonded woman?" I stomped around, snatching at bushes. How could he be so dense?

"Whoa. I sure she did, but…"

I whirled to face him. "But what?"

"I'm sorry. I know you know all that." He backed up and I followed. "But calm down. We'll make it." He reached out to me.

"Right," I snarled, and stalked off, not quite understanding why I was so mad at him.

#

At supper, Mama said, "Dear, we need to tell Judee, to warn her and her people."

"Oh. But he wouldn't have gone anywhere near them."

"We don't know how far their young ones wander. Sit here and we'll do it now, before Larry gets home."

Mama made contact and *told* Judee what I'd seen.

'We must meet, with daughters,' Judee *sent*.

We arranged to meet the next morning.

#

As Mama and I walked up the river bank to the crossing, I thought of the furry brown Wati who had taken Mama and her people with them when Judee and her people escaped their conquered world. Judee, their matriarch, was always in our thoughts, although she and Mama didn't get together very often any more.

We crossed the river in one of the little boats made from the crew bunks from Emprisa, our ship in orbit, to the croplands. Our meeting place was a large, flat meadow above the fields, where Judee could land her solar powered shuttle. Because the Bramites didn't trust the Wati, Judee refused to come to River Point.

At the meadow, we perched on one of the dirt filled rocks along the edge, and I listened to Mama pant. She needs more exercise, I thought. The sun felt warm on my face.

The silver shuttle swooped down and settled on the ground. The hatch swung down and three Wati descended. Judee wore her bright red and yellow meeting scarves. Being furry, they didn't wear regular clothes like us. The two others, one only half her size, wore pale yellow and white.

Mama and I stood and held out our hands. Judee leaned on the one who was her height.

"Greetings, Judee. How are your trees?" Mama asked.

"Greetings, Lyn. Trees are well. My daughters, Dela and Hori."

"My daughter, Perri," Mama replied. The meeting rituals complete, I stepped forward and looked at Judee's girls. They stared back until Judee nudged the taller one, who helped her to a seat next to Mama.

"After we talked yesterday, Dela tried to *reach* you. Did you feel it?"

"So that's what it was," Mama said. "I thought it was one of our little ones."

As Judee looked at her older girl, so did I. Dela had gray eyes, and I *felt* her discomfort and fear.

"Dela will *reach* for you or your daughter from time to time. All you need do," she swiveled her head to face Mama, "is to respond. Let her know if you understand, if strong enough." She rolled her 'r's.

"All right," Mama and I said together. Mama started to ask why. As we looked into Judee's great green eyes, we saw the dullness, and knew. I also noticed silver hairs in the brown fur.

"Yes, I am reaching the end of my years. I am training my second daughter, Dela, to take my place when I am gone." Hora whimpered.

"Second?"

"My first daughter remained on Wat to lead those who stayed behind." Her eyes closed, and I felt Mama's pang of sorrow. Mama had known Judee longer than anyone else except Uncle Adam and Papa, that she could remember.

Judee opened her eyes, looked briefly at Dela, then back to Mama. "She not ready yet; hopefully will be by the time I go."

"Mama," Hori whimpered. I *soothed* the little one as she tried to hide behind Dela.

"Dela will care for you if I go before you are grown." I *felt* Dela tense for a moment. "She may need your help, both you. Has your daughter mated yet?"

"She will be bonded in five days."

"Good. Dela is carrying first daughter in pouch."

"Pouch?" I asked.

Judee patted Dela's tummy. "Child tiny like this." She spread her forefingers about an inch apart. "Will grow in pouch for many days." She looked at us girls. "Now daughters, is time for you to learn each other. Dela, take Perri over there and tell her how we are arranged. Lyn and I will talk together."

"But I can't," I began.

"Use your head," Mama said. "She should know Standard."

As I followed Dela and her sister, I *reached* to Dela. 'I have no hearing,' I *sent*. She turned and looked at me, nodded, and continued to the end of the field.

'What you know of us?' Dela asked. I *heard* her in my mind. Hori started to say something, but Dela hushed her, and sat her down on a rock.

"Your mama saved my mama, you live in trees and eat plants, your people led by females," I said.

Dela nodded, and asked how we lived. We conversed, but I was aware that her mindlink was nowhere near as strong as mine, and wondered how she would *reach* us from her distant community. I prayed that Judee would live for a long time yet.

When she beckoned, we returned to our mamas. They had been reminiscing about the old days on Centralia, where they'd met.

"We can connect now, we have a link," I told them.

"Good," Judee said, and slipped down, her head on Dela's shoulder.

I *felt* Mama's fear, and said, "She's only sleeping."

"She sleeps much now," Dela said. "When she wakes, we return to Harmony Wat."

Mama's knuckle crept to her mouth. Judee was her oldest female friend. And Mama would be retired when I took over, not that I wanted to yet, and she would be the old auntie everyone went to for advice. Another Aunt Alice.

"Okay, Mama."

She smiled at me as we rose. We made our farewells and left. I thought of Aunt Alice, Doc Richard's wife. She'd been a nurse in her old Earth life, and had made many friends here among the Bramites. She'd taught health care and natural medicine, later taught new teachers. Now she was old, nearly bedridden, and many of the unbonded girls tended to her. Was that what Mama thought her life would be?

"Not for a long time," I said aloud. "You'll always be top Mama."

Chapter 9   Peter Disappears

At council, we discussed the Gates problem. Uncle Adam hadn't been able to find enough men who could be let off their duties for ten days, so the expedition to find the mountain Gate had been put on hold. Uncle Art had come up with a couple gadgets, and Uncle Allen and Art Junior had left for the Rock Gate.

Mama did insist on a rotating shift of two or three people, with at least one with Talent, to go up to the top of the trail every few days to *search* for anything unusual.

The next few days drove the Gates out of my mind as we finished up a lot of odds and ends from winter, and started preparing for the bonding ceremony and feast. Not to mention trying to finish our house. Several others were in the same situation.

On the morning of Bonding Day, I woke up in a puddle of mixed emotions. I would become a woman today, and move into my own house, where I could set up things the way I wanted. But Charley would be running our lives, and he was as bad as Mama at bossing me around. Once the ceremony was over, I could forget having anything to do with Gabe. Of course, he'd been bonded for years, but if I'd only had the chance…

Stumbling out of bed, I dressed, packed up my things, and took them over to my new house. I looked around, smiling. Pale yellow walls and only a bed and a table with two chairs made it look bigger than it was. A sink, counter, shelves, and cold food box in a back corner made up a kitchen. My kitchen, not Mama's.

I dumped my things on the table just as Charley arrived with his. He dropped his on the bed and grabbed me. "You ready, kid?"

"I guess."

After kissing me, he put his things away, some on the shelves, some clothes on the hooks. I piled mine in a corner on the floor.

"Come on, time to go," he said, looking scrumptious in a dark blue embroidered tunic and white pants.

I wore a long white tunic with lace around the bottom and sleeves, a necklace of shells and clay beads, and Grandpa's scarf.

"Something old and blue," Mama had said when she gave it to me. "And something borrowed."

Charley and I walked down together, hand in hand, and tiny flitterers stirred in my innards. I knew this is what we were always meant to do, but still it made me nervous. Others joined us.

Beth and Anne stood at the edge of the plaza directing traffic. "You look so pretty," Beth said.

"Over there, guys," Anne grinned, pointing to the side door of the meeting house, where the people being bonded were gathering.

"Next year," I said, as we moved on. I wondered if the other girls were as nervous as I was. They wore white or pale colors. We all looked at each other out of the corners of our eyes. Kareth came to stand with us.

At the sound of the gong, she began lining us up, Charley and me last. We walked through the door, along the side wall to the rear, then up the center aisle to the stage. Was this real? I saw Mama and Papa in the front row, Aunt Pauli and Uncle Bay next to them.

Tara, Kareth's mother, the oldest female in direct line from Bram, led the ceremony. Although her hair was white, few lines showed in her face. She smiled now, as she always did. She loved all the children, and delighted in performing bondings, as it meant more children.

She lined us up along the rear of the platform, facing her as she turned her back to the audience, so our families and friends could see our smiling faces. I fought to keep my smile in place. There were seven of us couples. She intoned the rites and said, "Now raise your joined hands and speak."

We all did so, and recited after her, "Caring forever, sharing forever, and many children."

"You are now bonded," Tara said. "You are excused until the feast." We filed off the platform and marched out, women smiling, men grinning.

Charley hurried me back to our little house. All I saw of it that afternoon was the ceiling. We just made it back in time for the opening of the feast, and weren't the last ones.

#

In the morning, I fixed breakfast, ate with Charley, dumped the dirty dishes in the washtub, and went to my class. When I came home, the dishes were still there, my night tunic still on the floor, and another bowl on the table.

I ignored them, got the packet of food Mama had left us out of the cold box, and read her instructions for cooking it. Charley came home and sidetracked me.

Later, after we ate, and I dumped more bowls in the wash tub, Charley said, "They won't wash themselves."

"Oh. Well, get me some water." He did, grinning, and I washed up the dishes, grumbling to myself. Now I was going to have to do this every day.

"Until the kids get big enough to do it for you," Charley said, still grinning. I could have punched him.

#

Several times in the next few days I started up the trail to Mama's before I remembered I didn't live there anymore. My little house kept me busier than I could believe. Not only did I have to clean it every day, I had to go pick up our food and whatever else we needed most days. And when Charley was home, he kept me busy in other ways.

One day Peter caught up with me as I was heading home. "Guess what," he said. "They're going to let me go up the trail tomorrow."

"No." Something like a black cloud surrounded me. A warning of dire danger. "You can't." I *sent* him what I'd felt. He shrugged it off.

"I know Mama and Papa have been keeping me home because they're afraid I'll run off or something, but I'm not, I just want to check on one thing, so it's okay." He spun around, ending up facing me. "So how's bonded life?"

"Fine. But please don't go tomorrow. Some other time, maybe. I've never had this bad of a feeling before. I don't want anything to happen to you." I reached my hands out to him.

"It won't." He jumped up and hung on a tree branch for a moment before he dropped. "I'll hook up with you when we leave so you can keep track of me. See you later." He loped up the trail to Mama's.

At home, still rattled by the bad feeling, I *called* Mama and *showed* it to her. 'I don't know what to do. He wouldn't listen to me.'

'I'll tell Larry and we'll keep him home.'

'Thanks, Mama.'

#

When Charley burst through the doorway and announced that he'd been selected to lead the group up trail the next day, I said, "Great." As he grabbed me, I added, "I thought they said they wouldn't take newly bonded people."

After several kisses, he said, "I'm the only one with Talent able to get off. Why great?"

"I just saw Peter and he said he was going. Mama and Papa are going to try to keep him home." The cloud turned gray. I told him about my feeling. "So if he does go, keep a close eye on him, will you? He wouldn't listen to me."

"Okay." He smiled down at me.

"He said there was something he wanted to check out, but wouldn't tell me what it was. He'll probably be okay until you get near the top."

Charley changed the subject.

In the morning, Peter *linked* with me. He'd managed to escape, I didn't ask how. 'Petey, please stay out of trouble and watch where you're going.'

A little later, Mama *called* to tell me he was gone.

'I know, we're linked. I told Charley and he'll keep an eye on him.'

'I certainly hope so.'

That afternoon, when I was cleaning up my classroom, I *sensed* Charley hollering, and *tuned in*. Peter was running up along the river bank above the trail, ahead of the others. 'Petey, come back,' I *yelled* at him.

"What's going on?" Mama came in. I *showed* her, and we both *yelled*. He kept going and Charley ran after him. And then his mind was gone. I could still *sense* his body running.

'"He's shut himself off," I said aloud. We switched to Charley, who was huffing and puffing, followed by Han, Uncle Adam's second son.

Finally Peter dropped in a little glade and the block was gone. He sat, head in hands, breathing hard. He still wouldn't listen to us. He could be as stubborn as I am.

As Charley and Han approached the glen, Peter raised his head, then jumped up and trotted on. The river and its banks curved sharply. He galloped around the corner and ran into something hard, not a tree.

We lost his link. He was gone, mind, body and all.

Chapter 10   Preparing to Follow

"No!" I screamed, and passed out. Mama's kisses brought me back, and I automatically *reached* for Peter before I was fully awake. Nothing, just an enormous emptiness, a gaping hole within me. Mama was saying something.

"Focus on what he ran into. Is it what you saw before?"

I obeyed. "No. That thing was much wider, and shiny, like metal. Nothing like us or Cray."

Uncle Adam and Gabe pounded into the room. "What happened to Peter?" Uncle Adam demanded. Gabe was as white as the sand outside.

"He's gone. Something ate him," I said. "Charley." We linked and I *felt* him shaking. Our Four had been torn apart. I *heard* Mama *telling* Uncle Bay and Aunt Pauli what had happened.

'It was a huge walking machine,' Charley *sent* to all of us. 'A door in its middle opened and sucked him in. Our link broke when the door shut. I couldn't get to him, I couldn't run fast enough.' I sensed him collapsing in a heap, his shoulders shaking.

'It's not your fault,' Mama *sent* to Charley, and the rest of us echoed it.

'Rest until you're ready to go, and come home,' Uncle Bay *added*. He unlinked.

"Gabe, walk Lyn and Perri home," Uncle Adam said. "I must think how to deal with this."

Mama and I were in a state of shock as Gabe took our hands and led us away. My brain whirled rapidly in all directions, and Mama had nothing to say. All my thoughts came back to Peter. He couldn't be gone, he was just hiding and he'd pop out any minute.

At Mama's house, Gabe put his arm around me and squeezed. "We'll get him back," he said, kissed my forehead, and left. I stared after him as Mama pulled me into the house.

"This can't be happening," she said, holding my hands.

"Everything's gone so well. You and Charley, all of the little ones, the whole community. Nobody can take my son away from me."

Something came to me from deep within. "Peter's not dead. We have to find him and bring him back."

"Do you *sense* him?" Mama said eagerly.

"No, it's deeper than that. It's in our twin connection."

"Bring him back from where?"

"Wherever that thing took him. Get a bunch of us to go after him."

"Oneness, help us find Peter and take care of him until we do," Mama cried, and collapsed on the couch, sobbing.

"Why did you let it take him?" I echoed, sitting beside her, dry-eyed.

Papa found us like that when he came home a little later. "What on Earth..." He scooped up Mama into his arms.

"Peter's gone," I said, and told him what happened.

"Jeesus Christ," he said, rubbing Mama's back. "I knew that boy would get into trouble sooner or later."

"Did you get into trouble much when you were a kid?" I couldn't help asking.

"Well, maybe one or two times. It's a boy thing." Mama made a choking noise. "How are you doing?" He looked at me over Mama's head.

"I feel like half of me is missing. I don't know what to do." I wanted Charley, but he wasn't here.

Mama sat up, still in Papa's arms. "You stay here," she said, "at least until Charley gets back." She closed her eyes, breathing fast. Finally she said, "I *told* Allen to set up an expedition to find the mountain Gate and any traces of that thing. Gabe will go. But not you. I know what you're thinking, and you're staying right here. But you can link with Gabe."

I wanted to do something, but there was nothing I could do right now. I huddled in the corner of the couch and let the tears come.

After supper, which only Papa ate much of, I tried to *reach* Charley and could not. Before I could say anything, Mama said, "He's up there, he's coming home."

"But," I began. Then, "I just realized, Mama, I have to go after Peter."

"No." Mama reached out for me.

"Mama, I have to. I'm the only one who can, because of our special link."

Mama refused to consider it, Papa said no, too. Finally I gave up and crawled into my old bed. I had to find Petey, not just for me, but for our Four. If we didn't get him back soon, we might not be able to relink our Four at all. And the community needed it, and him, too.

Because of our twin-link, once I went through the Gate, I should be able to *sense* and find him. I lay there and stared at the wall until Mama shook me awake in the morning.

It all came rushing back. She looked as awful as I felt. "What are we going to do?" I asked.

"Start by getting dressed." She sat on my bed. "Figure out how to deal with Peter. Get some clothes and things from your house. And we need to tell Judee and Dela about it."

Papa was beating up some eggs, but I wasn't hungry. Mama and I went out to the porch. "What do I tell her?"

"Just what happened, ask if they've seen anything, keep their eyes open, tell us if they do see anything."

"Okay, Mama." I sat on the porch chair and *reached* for Dela. "Mama, I can't reach her. Can you?" Together we did, and explained what had happened.

Dela told us of the youngster who'd seen someone above the trail. 'What are you going to do?'

'I don't know. Maybe go after him.' I took a deep breath. 'We need you to stress to your people the importance of keeping a lookout. If they find you, it could be dangerous for your people, too. Peter won't say anything, but we don't know what they could get him to tell. If you do see something, let us know. We'll keep in touch.'

She *said* she'd tell her mother, and cut off.

Mama and I looked at each other. "What happened to your Talent?" she asked.

"I don't know. Peter. I think our Talents overlap somehow and we were linked, so maybe he took part of mine."

"Well, that might help him, but it doesn't do you any good. Have you tried *reaching* Charley this morning?"

I tried, and could barely sense him. "He's there, but I can't tell where." It was a relief to get that much.

"Good. At least you still have some of your Talent."

She stood up. "I need to go to my class. It'll keep my mind off things. I hope. You needn't go, but you may listen in if you wish. There's mending if you want something to do."

Full of emptiness, I watched her march down the path. I knew she didn't want to be around other people yet, but she had her duties. I didn't really want to be with them either, but I was so alone up here. Linked with Mama, I could *sense* people, and who they were, mostly, but not what was going on with them like I usually did.

Mending wouldn't keep my mind off my missing link, even if I didn't hate it.

Papa came out of the house. "Hey, sugar, you going to be all right?"

"Yes, Papa." He kissed me and strode down the hill. I watched his stocky figure until he disappeared into the trees. He had no idea what Mama and I were going through, he had no idea of what it was like to have Talent. But he was a good dad, and he and Mama were inseparable.

I slouched into the house and dug out the mending and sewing kit. *Petey, where are you?*

After a while I *reached* for Charley.

'I'm here,' he *sent*. 'I can hardly hear you.'

'Where are you?'

'Too far away. I'll call when I get closer. Love you.'

'Love you too,' I broke the connection, slumped into the porch swing, and bawled my heart out. The first Four *came* to me, gently, led by Mama. They soothed my pain, even though they were all suffering too. Aunt Pauli relayed a message from Charley. He was coming home as fast as he could.

I slowly drew myself under control. I had to be in control to find Peter. But how? If he went through the mountain gate, would I have to go through that one too? Or did he? I sat up straight. What if the thing circled around and went down to the beach gate?

Since the machine showed up not long after Cray, would the gate still be set to his world? It only seemed logical that the machine man would have come from Cray's world. Two different people from two different worlds in such a short time seemed too improbable. What would come through the gate next?

I fought terror and grief.

Presently I picked out a sock, draped it over the darning egg, and threaded a needle. Setting my mind on pleasant things, like my baby, I still managed to ruin two socks and a tunic. I threw it all down and climbed up the ridge. After not finding the least hint of Peter, I closed down my mind and curled into a ball under a wide tree.

Eventually a question stirred me awake. Why did they want to capture Peter? Was it him in particular, or just whoever it came across first? What did Cray know of Peter, if anything, and how much had the mysterious 'they' gotten out of him? Why did it have to be Peter? Why not Han?

I sat up. Actually Han would have been worse in a way, because who would have gone after him? Mama and Papa and Charley wouldn't have let me, even if I'd felt the pull. Aunt Kareth couldn't, she didn't have the Talent to find him. Uncle Adam? Maybe. Gabe? I shook my head and started back down.

When Mama came home, she talked about her day a little, but I could feel her emptiness. "How are you doing?"

"Made three messes." I showed her what I'd done and she shook her head. "Mama, I've been thinking. I have to go through the Gate and find Petey. I can't live like this without him."

"No." She turned away from me and pounded on the table. "No you will not. Just forget about it." I knew she couldn't bear the thought of losing me, too, so I didn't say any more about it. But I still knew I had to go.

After supper I brought it up again. "We can't plan on them bringing him back," Papa said. "So we must send someone after him. And Perri is the obvious choice, having the closest link with him. If she goes through and can't sense him, she can just come back here."

Maybe, I thought. I knew how Mama felt, but the Gate pulled at me, even from there. "I need to go soon," I said.

"No." Mama held me tightly.

"You need to be prepared," Papa said, twiddling his spoon. "You can't just run off into the night. You need to plan what you're going to do when you get through the Gate, and..."

"I'm going to *reach* for Peter and go to wherever he is." I'd already thought about it.

"As I was saying, since we have no idea what it's like there, you need to take an assortment of things you might need. Lyn, get her a cloak with lots of pockets that she can carry things in."

"I've got a bag," I said.

"I'll get with Art in the morning to see what gismos he can come up with. Then we'll walk you up to the Gate the following morning."

"No," Mama moaned.

"I can't wait that long. He could be gone or the Gate closed by then."

"Don't you want to wait for Charley to get back?" Mama said. "He should be home by tomorrow afternoon."

"Yes, but…" I did want to see him before I left, to spend a night in his arms, but Peter… "Okay," I said finally.

The next day, which lasted forever, I hiked over to my house after breakfast and went through everything I owned. My to-go bag contained an extra tunic, my comb and toothbrush, and a little animal figure Peter had made me out of wires, nuts and twigs.

As I cleaned house, I *followed* Charley as he headed home, *sensing* him clearly now. After dinner, at home, I cleaned up there until I *sensed* he'd reached the top of the trail. I dropped my cleaning rag and ran out the door, right into Aunt Pauli's arms.

"Wooof," she gasped, dancing into balance. "Let's go meet Charley." We hiked up to the high trail and ran along it to where it joined the river trail.

"What happened to your Talent?" she asked.

"I don't know for sure, but I think some of it went with Peter. We were linked when he disappeared."

"Okay. Your mom and I have been telling people that he stayed up the trail and will go with Allen's group."

We met Charley about a third of the way up the trail. Gasping, he gathered me into his arms so tightly I could hardly breathe. Han panted down behind him a few minutes later. Aunt Pauli patted Charley's arm. He let me go long enough to give her a quick hug.

"My poor darling," he said to me, with a kiss. "I'm sorry, that thing was just too fast, and it didn't have to stop to rest."

I leaned against him, heart pounding. "Did it keep going straight up the river, or could it have started to curve to the west?" I asked him.

"The west? Oh, the rock Gate. It did seem to be getting farther from the river where it curved away to the south."

"Good." I looked up at him. "I have to go after him. I'm going in the morning."

"No," Aunt Pauli said.

"What? How?" Charley gripped my arms.

"Through the rock Gate. Mama and Papa are getting stuff ready for me."

"No. I need you here."

"You'd only have half of me. Anyway, I don't have a choice. You've felt what our Four is like without him. It'll die if I don't get him back."

"Then I'm going with you."

"No," Aunt Pauli repeated. "But we'd better get going back before people miss us." She started down.

"If Aunt Lyn can let her last child go, why can't you let me go?" Charley asked with a smile. "After all, I am a grown man."

Aunt Pauli stiffened, but said nothing. We continued down, took the high trail to Mama's house, and found her already home. Although I'd *felt* her with me, she gave off a great sense of relief. Uncle Bay was there, too, and gave us a big hug.

How could I leave her, and Charley, and all the others? But I had to, had to find Peter. "Aunt Pauli and I went up to meet Charley," I said. Han had taken the main trail into town.

"I know." Mama hugged me. To the others, "We have plenty of food, come eat with us."

"Thanks, but I must get home to the rest of my brood. Coming, Bay?"

"I think I'll stay here. Later." He kissed Aunt Pauli and she left.

Charley started to say something, but I cut him off. "Let's stay. I don't know what we've got in the pantry. Nothing seems real anymore."

As we ate, we made plans. Papa, who'd come home shortly after Aunt Pauli had left, had a long list of suggestions, and he presented me with a small pouch of goodies from Art. There was a little multi tool that had a knife blade, tweezers, screwdrivers. A magnet, a length of strong fine wire, some tape.

Mama pushed food around on her plate. I ate out of habit. "You need to eat, too, Mama," I said. I ignored Uncle Bay, sitting in Peter's place.

"You don't know what's out there," she said, picking up a small chunk of bread.

"Basics," Papa mumbled, and swallowed. "The alien apparently had no trouble breathing our air, so Perri should be able to breathe theirs. Gravity appeared to be similar. Judging from his clothing, the climate can't be much different. They must have mountains and rivers and places for people to live."

"True," Uncle Bay said, wiping his mouth. "As I see it, we have three choices. One, we sit here and hope they dump Peter back through, unharmed; two, wait until they send more aliens to capture or harm us; or, three, we let Perri go. I vote she goes. The aliens could come back and destroy us all, but if she, Peter, and her baby can get somewhere safe over there, the race can still continue."

I looked at him. "How did you know?"

"I saw it in you." He grinned.

"That's a good point," Papa said.

"Yes, but we're not going to be destroyed," I said. Just then, Uncle Adam dropped by to wish me well.

"Thanks, Uncle Adam."

Uncle Bay explained what we'd decided.

"Easy for you to say. She's not your daughter."

"I am now," I returned. "Anyway, I'll find Petey and bring him home." Suddenly my belly was full of flutters. How could I do it, go somewhere I knew nothing about?

Uncle Adam said farewell, and went on his way, accompanied by Uncle Bay. Mama began packing up food. I picked up plates and took them to the wash tub.

A little later, Mama showed me the bag of food and put it in the cold box. "I want you to take this." She took Grandpa's scarf from its hook and handed it to me. The scarf was the only thing left she had from her father.

"It's time to pass it on. Dad's a long way away now, but this links the generations. If you don't come back," she gulped, "it is to go to your first daughter and then to hers."

"Oh, Mama." I ran the blue and green swirls through my hands. Through my tears, the scarf seemed to be binding all of us together.

"It got me this far. Now it's your turn." She wiped her eyes. "Is there anything else you need?"

"At least I won't need period rags." We giggled a little, and I wrapped the scarf around my shoulders.

#

It was midmorning when we finally set off. Mama kept finding things she absolutely had to do before we left. Charley and I, Mama and Papa, Aunt Pauli, and Gabe made up our party. I stewed in an agony of impatience.

Charley handed me my cloak and bag, picked up his, said, "We're going," took my hand and pulled me out the door. The others caught up with us a few minutes later. Although I felt the pull from the Gate, something was also holding me back. None of us walked fast.

By the time the sun rode high, the pull was only from the Gate. We ate as we walked, even though Mama wanted to stop. I had to force myself to breathe and my heart to calm down. The closer I came, the worse the flutters became.

When we reached camp at the rock, even my hands were shaking. Mama and the others dropped their packs. I kept my eyes on the forest. If I even looked at the rock now, I'd start running for it.

"How about sleeping over and going in the morning?" Mama asked as the sunset faded into the sea.

"I couldn't sleep," I said. "I'm going now. I don't dare wait any longer." I felt Mama and her Four trying to calm me down. "I love you all." After hugs all around, I added, "I'll be all right, and I'll bring Petey home."

"I'll take care of her," Charley said, hugging his mother. Mama and Aunt Pauli clung to each other as we turned toward the rock. Charley held me to a fast trot.

I stared at the faint fog on top of it. At the base, Charley said, "Last chance to change your mind."

"Way too late for that." The pull from whatever was beyond the Gate enveloped me, growing stronger at every step. My anxiety and sadness at leaving my family grew fainter. By the time I reached the top, I was barely aware of Charley's hand slipping out of mind. I could only think of Peter and the others that awaited me.

The fog drew me in with a soothing embrace.

PART TWO – OTHER WORLDS

Chapter 11   Conception

LYN

I watched my little girl walk into the mist and disappear. Larry returned from down the beach and held me in his strong arms, his hand on my head. Somewhere in the back of my mind, I heard Charley said something about it not letting him through.

Pauli replied, and she and Charley murmured. I felt as empty as I had when I'd awakened on Ruthor without my memories. I had had nothing then, and I had nothing now.

I must have said it aloud, for Larry murmured, "You have us."

I looked up at his set face. "If I lost you, too, I'd blow away in the wind."

"You won't. The kids will be back," he said.

I *reached out* for the Four. Adam could not quite hide his pain. I realized how hard it had been for him all these years to be unable to acknowledge the twins as his children. If he hadn't already had Gabe and Amy…

As Larry led me to the campsite, I recalled the twins' conception. It had been Adam's plan, as directed by our father and the Watchers, for us to mate and produce the next generation of the new race of Talent. He'd known this for ten years before I showed up on his world, and he'd had to wait until we'd settled on our new world.

Blindly, I helped set up camp and supper, lost in my memories.

I'd known the moment Adam had told me I was selected for the next expedition that the time had come. The two of us, and Doc Richard and his wife, Alice, were to take a two day trek south along the coast.

Since I had never conceived with Larry, I knew this was the only way I could have a child. And I knew Larry would not be happy with it, although he'd known it would happen someday. So I waited until the evening before to tell him I was going.

He froze, his back to me, when I told him Adam had selected me to go. "I'm sorry," I said. "But he won't take no for an answer."

"Okay," he said, walked away, his fists clenched.

When the time came for me to leave, he held me tighter and longer than usual. "You're always my number one man," I told him, and kissed him. He let me go and stalked into the bedroom. I waited out front for Adam and the others.

I hated hurting Larry like that, but I also had chills thinking about Adam. As I walked with him, I felt his desire, and fought to keep my emotions under control. Scared, excited, and anxious, with a tinge of concern about Larry. He and I had been raised together as cousins; his mother had died shortly after his birth. Mom, his father's twin, was his mom, too.

Larry had always been there for me even though I couldn't remember it. He'd always been my best friend and protector. When my fiancé, Steve, died, and the Bramites required us to pick mates, it was only natural that Larry and I picked each other. I couldn't imagine life without him, and at least I still had him. But he could not give me a child.

Adam asked me, "How is the schooling going?"

"Very well. The children mostly enjoy it and are learning."

"Good. Do you know why I selected you this time?" We were well ahead of the others; we had to stop every now and then for them to catch up.

"I have an idea." My hand swung out and touched his.

"It is time, and it is our destiny. I have waited long for this, Lyn." Adam fiddled with his pack straps. I looked past him, at the sea lapping at the shore.

"You're lucky it's the right time of the month for me to conceive. You should have checked with me before you planned this."

"Oh."

Men never think of these things, I thought. "Did you tell Kareth I was going?"

"She does not need to know everything I do."

I snorted under my breath. *I bet she knows.* We walked on.

At our dinner stop, I was looking at some berries on a tree when Adam came up behind me. For a moment, his maleness overcame me, and I was ready right then. I controlled myself, and when we ate, I sat with Alice.

"Are you all right? You look a bit flushed," she said.

"I'm fine." I tried not to blush.

"It's all right, dear." She picked up a spoon. "I know the family must continue." Then I did blush.

That afternoon, I kept Adam at a distance. As we approached our camp site, butterflies began to flock in my innards.

After supper and an accounting of what we'd found that would be useful to the settlement, Doc and Alice laid out their blankets on the sand near a large tree. Adam led me down the beach to a cove out of the view of the others.

What I was most aware of then, was that he wasn't Larry. I was fired with desire, and Larry was nowhere around.

As Adam arranged the blankets, I went into the trees to empty my bladder. Inside, I felt split in two. On one hand, the practical side said this was necessary for me to have a child and continue the race, a simple procedure that would occur only once. On the other hand, the emotional side, there had always been a physical attraction, which I'd mostly sublimated, and a curiosity of what it would be like.

He drew me down, and it was beyond my imaginings. We'd blocked our links to others, but the combined sensations of feeling what I was feeling, what he was feeling, what he was perceiving of what I was feeling, was simply beyond words. I wished it could go on forever.

As we lay together, catching our breath, I felt Dad nearby.

'My children,' he whispered into our minds, 'my beloved children, take care of the new generation. Take care of each other until the time comes for you to join me in the Oneness. I love you both.' He faded away.

"Dad," I whispered.

"Did you hear?" Adam asked

"Yes." I turned to him, weeping. The worst part of losing my memories was not having any of Dad. He was so special and I would never know him.

Later, Adam snoring beside me, I tucked my feeling of guilt away with the memories of this wondrous event, and guided the sperm to my eggs.

When we returned to River Point, I was my usual cheerful self, but it took Larry five days to thaw out. By then, I knew I was carrying twins.

Chapter 12   Into the Mist

PERRI

I stepped into the mist, hands clenched and my whole body tingling. Another quick step to get away from the tingles, and more mist. Two more steps and still in the fog. Bluer and darker.

The others were gone. The world had gone quiet. What on Harmony was I doing? Except I wasn't on Harmony any more.

What's going on? What happened to the green? It had only been a thin layer when I put my head through before. I tried to turn around, but something held me facing forward.

"No," I cried. The force pushed me into taking a few more steps. The mist grew darker. It was all I could do to keep from turning and running back, but I knew that force wouldn't let me. Peter. I had to find Petey.

"Petey," I panted, and *reached*. Nothing. He must be here somewhere. My feet kept moving as it grew darker, and I stuck my hands out in front of me. It was as if I were possessed, but I couldn't *sense* anything inside me. The place was dead quiet. There was no one for me to hear through.

At least what I was walking on was flat and firm. I had no trouble breathing, when I remembered to, and the temperature stayed cool.

"Petey," I said again, hearing it only inside of my head. My hands swung out and touched slick firmness. I tried to turn, but the force wouldn't let me. Screams rattled around in my head. Moving on, I kept my hands halfway front and halfway sideways. A few steps later, I *sensed* vibrations in the air. Sound waves I couldn't hear. A great wave of scents followed, from flowery to five day old dead chicken.

I sneezed, and the scents faded out. The walls touching my hands went slick, sticky, hot, cold, furry, smooth, and back to slick. My hands moved out in front of me as the walls closed in.

I came to something solid in front of me, filling the tunnel. Pushing on it did nothing. My fists clenched.

"No," I panted. I'd seen a bit of a world before, why all this now? Whoever took Petey must be doing this, but why? In a sudden fury, I pounded on the wall in front of me, and it slid aside.

Before me stretched a room lit with late twilight dimness, lined with couches and chairs. Pictures dotted the walls, lighting up as I passed them. One with big red flowers caught my eyes for a moment.

Out of the dimness at the end of the place loomed a great head that looked like Uncle Adam with moving lips, but it couldn't be. I felt the vibrations again. The head was only a picture, I couldn't *reach* it.

After I stopped gawking, I put my hands over my ears and said, "I cannot hear." The lips kept moving. I repeated my words louder, felt something in my head, and I immediately shut down.

I shook my head and looked around. No windows, no doors, even the one I'd come in through was gone. A great desire to run home to Mama came over me, but I pushed it away. No way out, no way to find Petey, still no sentient beings. The face disappeared, replace by a picture of a stick figure climbing a rock and walking into mist.

"Oh, I did that," I said, taking a step back. What *was* this? My fists clenched, and the flitterers in my insides did a tap dance. Think, I told myself. Someone had made all these things. More pictures appeared, of all different places. Was I supposed to choose one? How?

"I need to find my twin, Peter," I said to the place. It began to move up and down, back and forth. "Oh." I stumbled toward a chair and was jerked onto a couch. I lay down on it, clutching the side. The last thing I saw was Peter's smiling face, firmly fixed in my mind.

#

Light in my eyes woke me up. I was still on the couch, but the mist and the shaking were gone. Directly across from me I saw a toilet through a half open door, and ran for it. When I emerged, I looked around. The place appeared to be the same, but something felt different. The air was warmer, and smelled more like flowers.

In the dead silence, everything looked flat. Halfway between the long side walls stood a round table bearing piles of what looked like food. Breads, fruits, bowls of grains and vegetables, other things I had no idea what they were.

I picked up a slab of bread and studied it. Not poisonous, but no nutrition for my body.

Dropping it, I went for a piece of Mama's bread. As I ate, a door opened in the wall where the face had been. I stuffed the last bite in my mouth, grabbed my cloak and bag, and trotted to the door. It opened wider as I approached.

The doorway led into a corridor with a dead end. I *reached* and found nothing.

There were doors along the corridor. The first one on the right opened onto a small bedroom with pale green walls and a coverlet with darker green trees. Beside the bed, there were a table and chairs, and a shelf with hanging hooks underneath. I saw no way out, not even a window.

The next door, on the left, opened into total blackness. I could *sense* nothing in there. The rest of the rooms along the right side were windowless bedrooms like the first one, in various colors.

I knew there must be a way out, but where was it?

The second door on the left opened to a blindingly bright light. I could *sense* nothing in there either. I found doors opening on solid colors I could not push through, and another room filled with blackness.

Getting madder and madder, I began to realize this was some sort of test. If that was so, then I was on the right world, the world where they'd taken Petey. That buoyed me up for a little while.

Finally I opened a door and saw outdoors. Steps down from a porch led to a red stone walk through a lawn to a double row of tall, narrow trees. As I started to step out, something made me stop and *reach*. There was nothing there, either, just a painted scene on something I couldn't push through.

"No," I howled, and stomped my foot. How could they do this to me? I knew I was in the right place, but I had to get out of here.

And then I saw one last door, right at the end of the hall.

This one opened onto a world of pale orange sand. I *checked* and it was real. But there was nothing but sand dunes, as far as I could see, in any direction. This was not like the world I'd seen in Cray's mind.

I stopped and thought. I knew there was no way out from any of the other rooms on this side, and the others were all windowless bedrooms. But maybe…

Back across the hall, I searched the gray bedroom thoroughly. I took the bed clothes off and peered under the bed. The floor was solid. I tapped all the walls and they all sounded the same. I could not reach the ceiling, but it appeared to be one solid slab. The shelf was solidly attached to the wall.

That left the sand dunes. Maybe there was something in back that I couldn't see. Well, here goes, I thought, and stepped out. After three paces, sudden dizziness attacked me and I fell to my knees, head down.

When my head cleared, I looked up and saw green hedges all around me. Now what? I *reached*. I *sensed* no danger, nor any sign of Peter, but a strangeness I couldn't understand. I turned around. There was a blank wall of hedge where the door had been.

I felt like Alice in Wonderland, a character in a book Aunt Alice had brought from Earth. Nothing was like what it seemed to be. Although I was shaking with terror, somewhere deep inside I knew I would find Peter.

I marched in between the hedges until I came to a place where another one split off to the left. Something about mazes tickled my brain, but I couldn't pin it down. I chose to go right.

Continuing along, every time I came to a branch I took the right one. Something in my brain was directing me. Then I came to a place where there were three branches.

Needing rest, I sat down and took out a hunk of bread. As I munched, I wondered what Petey would do. He was always climbing trees--that was it.

I tried to climb the nearest hedge in the corner between paths, but could not get high enough to see over the top. As I dropped down, I thought, I would have to find a sturdier one.

The rightmost path beckoned. The hedges grew taller, the sky darkened, and I was so tired I could hardly put one foot in front of another. How long would I have to go through this, I thought desperately. But I had to find Petey. I stumbled and fell.

Chapter 13   On the Trail

When I awoke, I found myself in a little circular nest made of some soft pinkish material. Sitting up, I saw I was on a wooden porch leading to a leaf lined path into a forest. Gates to each side blocked the walkway along the building. At least I was out in the open now.

The first thing I did was to *reach* for Peter. I *found* faint signs of sentience far away. Could one of those be Peter? I trotted down the path into the trees. These had rounder leaves than the ones I knew, but they were still trees.

I walked until I was too tired to go any farther. Just then, the path entered a tiny glade with a trickle of water. I collapsed and drank. A small patch of yellow flowers grew at one side. Stretching out on the ground, *I reached* again. The sentience was a little stronger, but I still couldn't pinpoint Peter. However, I knew he was there, and all I had to do was to keep going until I found him.

I slept well that night.

#

When I awoke, the little flowers had folded up in the dim light. The patch of sky overhead glowed dark blue. I wrapped my cloak around me and started out. In the forest, I had to go slowly because it was still dark under the trees and hard to see the path. Light around me gradually grew brighter as I marched on.

Alone on a strange world, I should have been petrified, but I wasn't. Somehow there was a feeling of a vast, encompassing protector. The Oneness? Somewhere underneath I knew I would survive.

Under the trees grew bushes with tiny white flowers, and others with long twisted brown pods. The path was covered with leaves and pods. Since I couldn't hear, I set my movement sensor on high and looked around a lot.

Little orange and blue creatures fluttered around on wide, colorful wings. I liked this place, but Peter always hovered in the back of my mind.

Near the end of the day I found another glade and prepared to camp for the night. A tiny light blinked across the way. I thought of fireflies that Papa had told me about.

#

The next morning, I woke to find myself in a dark, dank place that smelled of spoiled chicken.

"What?" I said, trying to sit up. I couldn't move. "No," I screamed. Not again. I forced myself to calm down and *reach*. This place was another façade. Maybe if I moved slowly...

My right forefinger moved, and then the others. Slowly I made a fist. After repeating with my left hand, I moved my hands out. Something like water but not wet surrounded me. My hands pushed through, I tore it open, and was sitting in the glade.

"All right, that's enough of that," I said loudly, getting to my feet. I stomped around. "Petey," I said, stopping and *reaching*.

I found a mass of people, and thought Peter was among them. Grabbing my cloak and bag, I marched off. In the back of my mind I wondered why they were testing me. Somehow I knew that's what they, whoever they were, were doing.

The following morning, I woke to the glade I'd collapsed in the night before. "So either they heard me, or they got what they wanted," I said, as I prepared to leave. More angry than scared, I realized that I had left the child Perri back on Harmony.

Two more days of trees and glades, punctuated by small groups of yellow flowers and unfamiliar but pleasant smells, brought me to the edge of the forest. Each day the sentience was stronger, but I was still unable to pick out Peter. My quest kept me from feeling lost.

A meadow of multicolored flowers stretched out in front of me. What looked like fields of crops and large beasts lay beyond. Past that, I saw rows of houses and taller buildings, masses of them, more than I could comprehend. Mountains ran along to my left, circling behind the buildings. To the right, the land stayed flat, and I thought I *sensed* a distant sea.

The path split, and I decided to take the one to the right. It took me in and out of the edge of the trees. In a thick, gloomy glade, I tripped over a fallen log, fell slowly, and landed on my knee instead of my face. After a short period of dizziness, I continued on. I'd have to be more careful, I thought.

When the path led me out of the trees, the sun had moved. It had been in my face before; now it was behind me. I stopped and looked around. The fields and the buildings were still there, but they'd moved over to the right. I took a step forward and stared at mountains.

"Oh no," I said. Somehow I'd gotten on the wrong path. I turned to go back the way I'd come, but the path ended at the trees. I couldn't go in there without a trail to follow, I'd never find my way out. There was a drop of about house height to the meadow. I didn't dare try to climb down there and risk an injured ankle or worse.

I turned again and headed toward the mountains. Every so often I stopped and *reached*. I found only more distant sentience, but still could not pinpoint Peter.

The road curved away from the trees, a narrow way between drop-offs on either side. Far in the distance a group of trees huddled beside the road. I plodded on, thinking about Charley, Mama and the others, wondering whether I'd ever see them again.

By the time I came to the small grove, I was ready to drop. There was a little spring, which I was very glad to see, and a place to lie down under the trees.

Once again I *reached*. Not only did I *sense* people in the buildings, but there was also something ahead of me, flickering in and out. If there were people there...

I ate the last of Mama's food and drank two cups of water. Curling up into a ball, I slept, and dreamed of Petey.

The next day I grabbed a handful of grass to munch on, and marched onward. Again, as I *reached*, the sentience behind me grew fainter and the one in front of me grew. As the trail began to curve toward my right, I began to sense moving things to my left. Topping a small hill, I saw large roundish blue and green machine-like things rushing past, much faster than I could run.

Later in the day, I came to a grassy place dotted with tables and benches, and a small building at the side away from the road. Round trees shaded the tables, and I dropped down at one and laid my head down on my arms.

I was so tired I could barely move, too tired to feel my hunger. My sweaty, sticky body demanded a bath. My Talent barely functioned, but I did *sense* sentient beings not far away.

My mind told me Peter was out there, and I wanted to jump up and run to him. I couldn't move, and Papa's words came back to me.

"Take it easy, sugar. You're the only one who can take care of yourself. Stop for the night when you feel tired, don't wait until you're about to drop. Pace yourself, you don't know how far you'll have to go. It won't do Petey any good when you find him if you're too sick to help him, or to find your way back."

I sighed, ate the last few crumbs in the bottom of my bag, and curled up in my cloak. Papa was right. He was always right.

Chapter 14   Ride to City

The next morning, I woke as it was starting to get light. I wandered around a bit, hungry and thirsty and with no desire for another long walk. I went over to the building. A little black bowl bubbled water. After tasting it and finding it good, I drank until my thirst was gone.

That helped, but I still couldn't get my feet to move. Dropping to the ground by a tree, I wrapped my cloak about me and slept.

#

I awakened to shaking. I found myself buckled into a seat in a moving box. In front of me, a very wide trail stretched ahead. Those blue and green machines rushed along it in the opposite direction. My tired, sleepy mind couldn't make any sense of this.

Out a side window, the world rushed by much faster than I could run. Turning my head the other way I saw a woman sitting beside me.

A narrow woman in a blue dress with tiny yellow flowers on it was moving a fat stick around.

"Um," I mumbled. Was this a dream?

She looked at me and her lips moved.

I *sensed* her mind full of words I couldn't understand. What if she didn't know Standard?

Her lips continued to move. I put my hands over my ears and shook my head. Waggling her shoulders, the woman turned to face forward.

My stomach growled. She glanced at me briefly.

As my mind reached full alertness, I realized that there were many buildings along the trail. In the nearest one, I *sensed* feelings, pictures of things I could not identify, and words I didn't understand.

I *reached* and found Petey, although I couldn't pinpoint his location or *touch* him. I knew now we were in one of the traveling machines and wondered whether the woman was taking me to him.

As we drew closer, I shut down my mind against the noise of many minds, keeping only a tiny wisp open for contact with Peter. What ifs sprung up. What if she went past the buildings? What if she took me somewhere and locked me up? How was I going to communicate with these people if I didn't know their words?

I knew I could find Peter from our link, but I was also *sensing* many dangers in this place. As I sat there watching the colored machines zoom by, I began to realize the enormity of the quest I'd set out on. And I understood better how Mama had felt when she was on her own quest.

"At least I know where to go to find Peter," I said aloud.

The woman glanced at me, and turned onto a side trail. Here there was an open space with grass, tall trees, and a rainbow of flowers. I relaxed a little. We were still going the right way.

Back in among gray buildings, after a few more turns, the woman slowed the machine and pulled into a cave under a taller building. She stopped the machine and the vibrations ceased. She opened a door in the side of the machine and stepped out. I found a handle, pushed, and a door opened on my side. I climbed out and looked around.

She came around the machine, took my arm, and led me through this open space under the building filled with dozens of these traveling machines, over to the side. We came to a tiny room big enough for about six or eight people squashed together. Inside it, I felt movement, and she patted my hand. I gasped at the smell, a combination of man sweat and musty flowers.

It stopped moving, the door slid open, and other people got on. Women in bright colors, men who looked like Cray in grays and browns. After two more stops, the narrow woman led me out and down a tan hallway with lots of doors. She tapped on one, and when it opened, she led me inside.

She said something to a woman in yellow sitting behind a table. That woman, with gray hair and bluegreen eyes, spoke to me, and I shook my head. She waved me to a big stuffed chair and I sat down. The room had one window, which I couldn't see out of, and shelves of books and figurines. As the two talked, I tried to *sense* what they were talking about. Me.

The flutterers were back. What were those women going to do with me?

I was much closer to Peter now, but something kept us from linking. He was in another building not too far away. I had to get out of here and find his building. The two women talked on and on. Finally the narrow woman departed, and gray hair rose, pointed at me to stay seated, and left through another exit.

I jumped up and ran out into the hallway toward the little moving room at the other end. The narrow woman had disappeared. There was a window at the end of the corridor, and I peered out. All sorts of boxes of different heights lay below me, with forest in the distance and mountains beyond.

A man appeared down the hall, coming toward me. I pushed at a door nearby and found myself in an enclosed space with two platforms. As I stepped back on one to let the door close, the platform began to sink. I clutched the center pole with both hands and prayed to Oneness to help me. Fortunately the platform didn't sink very fast.

When it stopped, I opened the door in front of me a crack and peered out. A wide open space stretched before me, with clear walls and what appeared to be an entrance on the far side. People hurried back and forth. A group nearby surged into an open little room like the one I was in. I crept out and trotted across the space as if I belonged there, shaking inside. No one stopped me. Outside, I turned away from the entrance, to stop beside a potted plant.

This place was utterly strange to me. This plant with droopy leaves and tiny blue flowers, almost as tall as me, was the only green thing I could *sense*, among all these buildings and machines. Everything inside me screamed to get out of here, except the link to Peter.

I checked Peter's location and headed in that direction. When I arrived at a corner where two machine trails crossed, I watched the other people and followed them over to the other side when the machines stopped. At least there was some sort of order here.

Crossing two more trails, I reached the square gray building that held Peter. The entrance, outlined in silvery strips, was set back into the side of the building, with wide, clear doors that slid open as I approached.

I stopped and stared, entered, stepped to the side, and *searched* for Peter. He was down below my level, but I wasn't sure how far down. And I still could not communicate with him.

Chapter 15   Perri and Peter Unite

"I'm coming, Petey," I whispered, and followed a group through the doors. It was like the other building; the front and sides of the great open area were glass, there was a low wall with a few openings, and back beyond that, a row of doors.

I watched for a bit and saw that the people going through the openings touched little square things to the top of the wall. Others were taking the things out of their pockets or bags as they approached the wall.

Well, I can't get in that way, I thought. "Petey." I blinked back tears and moved toward the side, where two women came through another outside door. If there were two entrances here, maybe there was another one on another side of the building.

I hurried out and walked back along the building. At the next trail, I turned right along the back, where I found a large flat door. I could not open it, so continued on and around the next corner. Half way along, I saw metal steps coming down the outside that ended at a door well above my head.

Waiting until there were no people close by, I jumped, and just managed to catch the edge. The steps slowly dropped down. When they stopped, I climbed up to the door. They crept up behind me. The door opened, revealing a small space with steps going up on one side and down on the other.

I started down. Every time I came to another door, I *reached* for Peter, until I found his level. He was on the other side of the building. This hallway had big open doorways showing machinery on one side, and small rooms on the other. I followed the hall until someone yelled.

Ducking into the nearest little room, I tripped over a bucket. There were piles of buckets, brooms, bottles, and mounds of cloths. It must be a cleaning room. It would take a lot to keep this big place clean. A tiny window let in a faint light.

I yawned. My body cried out for rest and sleep. I sat down on a pile of cloths. My eyes would no longer focus. I lay down on my side, cloak wrapped around me.

Sometime later I became aware of movement, of being carried, but I could not wake enough to find out more. When I was able to open my eyes, I was in a room like the first one, back before the forest. I sat up on the couch, blinking. Before I could think of anything else, I *reached* for Peter.

He was in the room next to mine. "Petey," I screamed, jumping up and pounding on the tan wall between us. I felt the wall vibrate, but heard nothing. I pounded three fast, three slow, three fast. One thing I'd learned early was SOS. But why couldn't I link with him?

'Perri, is that you?' faintly touched my mind. 'Something in wall.' A pause, as if he were catching his breath. 'How did you get here? Where are we?'

"In a big building in a bunch of big buildings. Did you see it?" I yelled. Again, I barely heard his answer.

'Machine let me out right outside door and shoved me in room. Lots of machinery and walls and people above.'

"I can't keep yelling." I laid my head against the wall. I could touch him if it wasn't for the wall. "We've got to get out of here." I felt agreement, then nothing.

I sat down, gasping, tears running down my face. I'd found him, but I couldn't reach him, in either meaning of the word.

He'd been here several days; if there was a way out, he'd have found it. I got up, I had to pee. I went around the room, opening cupboard doors, pounding on the wall, a long blue button.

A sanitary room appeared, and I used it with relief. A sink provided wash water and a bar of soap. I tore off my clothes and washed my body as best I could. As long as water came out of the faucet, I kept washing. I pulled down the drying cloth and soon felt much better.

Dressed and back out in the main room, I found food in one of the cupboard. This bread seemed to be all right. Peter had been eating it, since he hadn't anything on him when he was captured. At least we had the basics.

As I gobbled bread, I noticed that there was no door. "There has to be one, how else would I have been put in here?" I said aloud.

After I finished eating, I poked around a bit, and dug out my pouch of goodies. None of the blades would scratch the wall between us.

'Corners,' came faintly from Peter. I guess he could hear my scratching.

After much searching, I found a dent where a built in chair back met the wall. I jabbed at it and a little piece fell off. In a frenzy, I jabbed and pounded, and Peter pounded back. Finally the blade went through.

'Good,' Peter said, a little more clearly than before.

'There's a wall behind it.' I was able to *reach* him more easily, now.

'Smooth or rough?'

'Not as smooth as my wall. Let me see.' I pounded chips off the edge, enlarging the hole. Inside, I poked around and found a place I could scratch at. I felt Peter pounding with me, and broke through. There was still a wall between us, but now we had a full link.

We *meshed*, and each of us knew what the other had been through the last several days. I learned that his room had no door, and that food appeared in the cupboard when he was asleep. He also told me that, once in a while, different voices would say things in languages he didn't understand.

'There's one person nearby, maybe you can get something out of him.'

I relaxed. 'It's a different world, with a different language. I can sense feelings, and sometimes, pictures.' I tugged a curl. 'We got in here, there has to be a way out. We need to find it.'

'What do you think I've been doing for the last three days?'

'Oops.'

'The walls and floor, cupboards and furnishings are all one piece. They took my knife. What tools do you have?'

'Uncle Art gave me some stuff, knife, scissors, screwdrivers. Oh yes, a magnet. Let me try that person you mentioned.'

I *reached*. Quite close, a male sat at a table, doing something with a device in front of him. All I could *sense* was he was a guard. Not too far away, on the same level, were two more people who seemed to be bored. I moved up, and found many more people on many levels. The discomfort shut me down.

These people had held Peter for days. Why hadn't they done anything except feed him? Why would they come and grab him, and then just let him sit here? It didn't make sense.

We stayed linked, and talked now and then. Every so often I jumped up, yelled and pounded on walls. It only brought grins from Peter.

#

When I woke the next morning, I thought, what are we going to do when we get out? Could we just walk out of the building?

I sat up and *reached* to Peter.

'We'll worry about that later,' he responded. 'Did you say you had a magnet?'

'Yes, why?'

'Try moving it along the wall at different levels. I'll watch from this side.'

I didn't see what a magnet could do, but followed his instructions. Hunger nagged at me by the time we covered the wall between us, with no results.

'Try the short wall by your couch,' he said. I did, and half way up, a quarter of the way across, something clicked.

'Did you hear that?'

'Yes. Push up or down or sideways.'

I pushed out, then side to side. Nothing. Down, nothing. Then up--and the wall moved. As soon as I stopped pushing, it slipped back down. 'It moved up, Petey.'

'I know. Push it up again and I'll see if I can hold it up.' I did and he did, briefly. I saw the bottom of a door behind it.

'The whole room moved up, except the floor, and there's a door behind,' I said.

'There's got to be a mechanical way of moving it. Go take a nap or something while I figure this out.'

'Peter, I just got up.' I *sensed* his grin. I had some breakfast, and wandered around a bit. Finally I sat down with my back to his wall, and *reached* out. The same three were on our level, but a different one sat in the nearest place. Up a level were more people doing things I didn't understand. Focusing on one or two at a time as I worked up the levels, I found that many higher up were doing some kind of writing or number work. Some were looking forward to a time when they could go away from there.

And then I *found* him. Cray. He sat at a table working some kind of little machine--and thinking of me. There was the trail, the trees, and me. Dare I let him know I'm here? Can he help us, or would it make things worse? He picked up another device and put it to his ear. I decided to leave him alone for the time being, but I wanted to dance a jig because I'd found him. So this was his world.

Above the top layer was an area I could not penetrate. It was like a wall in a cabin next to a doorway. You could walk through the doorway easily, but the wall stopped you flat. I had a feeling that the people in charge of this place were in there.

Outside this building were more people, some in other buildings, others outside or riding in the traveling machines. No one seemed to know about us, except the three on our level. Only a few, such as Cray, had any kind of mindlink ability. And there were more people in this one building than in my whole settlement.

Overwhelmed, I shut down except for Peter. I thought about my little house and Charley, Mama and the others. What were they doing? Oh, for a tree to sit under. A thud from next door brought me out of my reverie.

Chapter 16   Escape

'Just me,' Peter said. 'Your magnet unlocked my door, too. Get your things, go to where you saw the door, and as soon as you see it, push it out and get out.'

I packed up as much food as I could stuff in my bag. He'd never think of it, but he'd be hungry later. The walls, including the furniture attached to it, crept upward. At first I thought the floor and I were dropping, a weird sensation.

When I saw the bottom of the door, I pushed it open and wiggled through. I barely noticed the thud behind me as Peter gathered me into his arms. I *felt* his anguish and relief, mingled with my joy and pleasure. At last we were together again. We were one. My full Talent was back.

I pulled away to look at him. He was even skinnier than when I last saw him, but a big grin lit his face. "Hey, sis, you're looking good. Let's get out of here."

He led me to a door at the end of the hall, past two rooms beyond mine. We peered through a little window and saw two men looking at something on a table, backs to us. Peter tugged me the other way. Two more rooms past ours, the hall turned to the right.

There we found a little room that moved. I explained it.

"Lift," Peter said. We entered, and it immediately dropped. When it stopped, the back slid open and Peter stepped out, onto nothing. I grabbed him and steered us over to a narrow walkway at the side. It led downward, rock wall on one side, bottomless drop off on the other.

"Oof," Peter said, clutching at the wall. I leaned against it next to him, trying not to pass out. "Great way to get rid of unwanted people."

After a while, we edged our way down until we came to a wider area where we could sit down. The rock wall curved over our heads to the other side of the crevasse.

Faint light a long way away allowed us to see a little. I didn't like this at all, but we had no choice but to go down. I could no longer *reach* anyone in the building.

At least we were together. I leaned against him. "How are you doing?"

"Better. How did you do that?"

"My Talent. It took a lot out of me. I need to rest for a bit."

"Okay. I don't know where we're going, but we're on a grand adventure together."

"Yes, but we need to get back home, to mend our Four."

Presently, we climbed to our feet and continued on down. The light brightened, and led us around a curve. The roof faded away, but the rock walls remained. It was chilly there and I wrapped my cloak around me.

Peter trotted down ahead of me. "Wait," I called. I still felt emptied out after saving us from falling, and could only walk slowly. The path curved out of sight. 'Peter, wait for me.'

Our link faded, I could barely sense him. Surely he'd notice I wasn't near him and come back for me. I plodded along the twisting, turning path. The wall on the other side dropped down to nothing as the crevasse filled in, revealing forest. I took a deep breath of real air, and *reached* for Peter.

In front and to my left ahead of me, he did not respond. My Talent was shot again. I followed the trail along the base of the cliff, constantly looking around and trying to sense movement. The ground sloped away through the trees, and the cliff curved across the trail, ending it.

"No," I cried, and leaned against the cliff. Peter had gotten out. How? I sniffed around, and found his scent between two bushes. I pushed through. Beyond the open area in front of me was a wider trail.

I plodded over to it and stopped. It slanted up to the top of the cliff to the right, and down the other way. Footprints in the dirt told me Peter had gone down, so I followed him. The Gate is really hidden up there, I thought, as I looked back and saw only trees.

Where was Peter? I was madder at him than scared of being alone. At a wide place I found a wooden bench and sat. A broad valley spread out below, split by a wandering river. Trees lined it and were scattered on the hills. I saw a few houses here and there. So there were people here.

I *reached* for Peter again and found a faint something down below. Why couldn't my Talent behave itself? I'd never get it under control. The sun warmed me. It felt good. I took off my cloak and started down. Bushes with small white flowers and a not very pleasant scent dotted the inland side of the trail.

Because I could not hear, and my Talent was wrung dry, every so often I stopped and turned back to see if anyone was behind me. I didn't want to meet any of the natives until I was back with Peter.

I found him waiting at an overlook near the bottom.

"Took your time, didn't you," he said, grinning. "I knew where you were all the time."

"I didn't know where you were," I yelled at him. "My Talent is practically dead and I can hardly walk." I collapsed on the bench beside him. "Don't ever leave me like that again." I leaned back, closed my eyes, and drifted into to a doze. I felt him rubbing my shoulder.

"Sorry, Perri."

Some time later I awoke, yawned, and stretched.

Peter sat up beside me. "Are you ready to move on?" he asked.

"Yes." I heaved myself to my feet. "Where are we, anyway?"

"On another world. Heavier. Look down there." He pointed. In an arc of the river lay a small circular village, with a canal completing the circle of water. In the open space in the center stood a larger building. Little bridges connected the village with crop fields outside the waterways. A road followed the river, going through the town.

"We have to go down there and find out how we can get back to our world," Peter said.

"Yes, there has to be another Gate on this world, but how are we going to find it?"

We plodded down to where the path joined the road above the village. As we crossed the bridge into the community, a small boy ran in between two houses, babbling something we couldn't understand.

A pair of women appeared, much shorter than I, wearing long brown dresses and their dark hair piled on their heads. One said something. We just shook our heads. They took our hands and drew us into the open center area. A line of bins stretched along a wall of the big building.

At each one, we stopped, and the women reached in and pulled out different items. Baskets, food, clothing.

Even though I didn't know whether we could eat them, I accepted a basket of fruits and some long thin sticks of bread. After that, we came to a water pump at the base of the second bridge.

I sipped. It was good. We drank, and I filled my water jug.

"Gates?" Peter asked. The women shrugged and pointed at the bridge.

Okay, I thought, climbing over the bridge. They're willing to share with travelers, but don't want us hanging around.

"Those bins are like our warehouse, but they don't have to sign things out," I said.

"Yeah, but there's lots more of us."

We continued on down the road, a line of trees between us and the river. Later, we stopped in a grove to rest and eat. I wanted to stay there, but Peter said, "We need to travel as long as there's light. Who knows what'll be there in the night."

Chapter 17   Cray

Cray had been content with his life until he'd met the alien. Now he could not get her face out of his mind. Unlike the round, brown, stubby-eared animal he'd seen first, the alien with the squarish face, black curls and tan skin like his fascinated him. She had helped him with his injured foot, and had not been afraid of him.

The others told stories of cringing natives, but he was glad she hadn't been like that. He'd heard and seen much about various aliens on other worlds, but never one like this. A young female here would never be allowed alone on a mountain trail, or anywhere else.

His mate, like all the other females, worked at the nursery and schools, caring for the young. When their youngest reached school age, his mate would become a teacher or other caregiver. He was proud that he had five offspring; that made him a top level male and enhanced his career.

Cray completed a batch of papers, stamped them, put them aside and reached for another stack. The other thing he kept thinking of was that the alien was mind aware. Very few of his people were; he was one of the favored ones.

Because he'd been chosen to learn the Gatekeepers' language, he knew more about them than most of his people.

A thought came to him. The alien had known of the brown faces, as equals.

Therefore the brown faces were more than mere animals. He'd not told anyone about the mind link, and it had not registered on the recording device. But if the brown faces were sentient, it was his duty to pass that information on to his superiors.

Cray set down his writing tool, remained still for a moment, and rose. His direct manager, Gorn, was not impressed.

"How is it you only now remember?"

"No one asked."

"You know you tell all, every little thing. Go tell Overmanager Dree. He will pass on your information. I'll notify him."

"Yes, Overone." Cray turned and marched out. He was not surprised by Gorn's lack of interest. He only cared about his numbers.

Upstairs in the Overmanager's office, he was left standing and ignored while OM Dree finished writing something. Cray stared at a wall depicting a forest of vines and gaudy red flowers, unlike anything he'd seen in a living woodland.

OM Dree looked up. "So you think brown creatures may be sentient. How?"

"Animals freeze or back away. This did neither. Its eyes appeared to widen. I thought I best report it."

"Good. Sometimes one thinks of things after the fact." OM Dree doodled on a pad at the side of his desk. "That would mean there are two sentient races on one world. Most unusual. Do you think they know of each other?"

"Yes. I saw them only a few hands of minutes apart."

OM Dree looked up at Cray. "How alien was the other?"

Cray wondered why he was asking; surely he'd seen the reports. "Much like us, smaller, green eyes, tan skin."

"So we could fit in with them."

"Yes, if the one I saw was shorter than most. But if there's not very many people, wouldn't they all know each other?"

"There is that." OM Dree twiddled his writing tool. He stared at Cray, who felt his mind link. "They don't have that many. Gatekeeper had a flyspeck sent in, which found a small community at mouth of river. Buildings amongst trees, light haired people, no large beasts. This is not to go beyond this office."

"Yes, Overone."

OM Dree smiled at him. "I may need to see you again in regards to this. You are very observant. You may go back to your duties."

As Cray returned to his cubicle, he thought about OM Dree's interest in this particular world. He'd only met OM Dree a few times, but he was much easier to work with than Gorn. He was actually interested in something outside the building.

The next day, Cray felt the alien's brief touch. How could she be here on Oron? She was on a low level, but he could not come up with a reason to go down there.

A few days later, he was called to OM Dree's office. A Gatekeeper, all in black, stood at the window behind OM Dree's desk.

"There are aliens down below," OM Dree said. Cray knew he meant the holding cells. "There were. They've just left through the cells Gate. We have chosen you to go after them and bring them back, if one of them is the one you saw. This Gate goes to village world. There will be some provisions, but take what you need. Return Gate is at mouth of one of the rivers. Go now, eat, pack, report to main Gate below."

"Yes, Overone." Cray returned to his cubicle to close it up, then to his quarters nearby. He hid his joy deep within. This was what he'd wanted, and he already knew one of them was his alien. He only briefly wondered who the other one was.

Chapter 18   Village World

PERRI

As we plodded down the river road, I said, "It seems to be getting dark earlier than it should."

"Could be they have shorter days here. Let's keep on until we can't see any more."

Hiking along the road past scattered clumps of trees on one side, and the burbling river on the other, reminded me of home. A stab of pain twisted my gut. "Mama," I whimpered, and touched Peter. At least he and I were together, wherever we were. Only we had no idea how to get home. All we could do right now was to continue to move forward.

Peter put his arm around me. "We're awfly far from home, aren't we?" he said. I *felt* his homesickness.

"Just don't go off and leave me again," I said, blinking away tears. He gave me a squeeze.

Darkness drew in around us, and I looked about for a place to camp. Then light drifted in from the river. "Is that a moon?" I peered upward.

"No, a boat. Come on." The light from the boat let us see the road as long as we could keep up with it, as it drifted on the current. When the boat picked up speed, we stopped and looked for a place for the night. A nearby grove provided shelter.

The sun was halfway up the sky when we woke up. We gobbled down some food, grabbed our stuff, and hurried on. Around midday, which felt like midmorning to us, we passed through another circular village and acquired more food and water.

Later, the river curved, and the road with it. Dainty breezes dusted off the sun's heat. Through Peter, I heard the forest and river songs, and a few times we saw small brown and white creatures hop away into the trees.

At the full dark of night, Peter insisted we stop and sleep, even though we weren't ready to rest. "We need to get into sync with this place while we're here."

As I lay listening to Peter's faint snores, I thought about our journey. If we found a Gate, would we be able to get through it? And to our world? I didn't even want to think about the possibility of having to raise my child with only Peter to help. Although, I supposed, there were a lot of worlds worse than this one.

I opened my mind. There was no danger near us, and the people in the nearest village were simple peasants. But there was something underneath I couldn't reach, something left over from the other world, something not good for our community.

Peter shook me awake shortly after the sun rose. I wanted another couple hours of sleep, but he insisted we get going. It was another sunny, warm day brushed with breezes. We passed a large bush with red and yellow flowers, and an unfamiliar flowery scent.

"Isn't that pretty," I exclaimed. Peter picked a red flower and tucked it in my curls. We continued down the path shaded by silvery trees, the river burbling away along at our right.

I *reached* every so often, but found only animal life.

From time to time, Peter kicked a pebble or swung from a low tree branch.

"Getting bored?" I asked.

"Sort of." He pitched a stone between two bushes into the river. "The walking is okay, but I wish I knew where we're going."

"Me, too." I touched a yellow leaf on a nearby bush. "But what else can we do but keep going?"

Peter shrugged.

About midday we came to another village and collected more food and water. At least we didn't have to worry about that.

At the bottom of the second bridge, a small dock with a blue boat tied to it sat in the water. A man nearby gestured at us, and then at the boat.

"He wants to know if we want a ride," I said, *seeing* a picture of us sitting in it and moving down the river in the man's mind.

"Is it safe?" Peter asked, looking at me.

"I don't sense any danger, I replied. I *sent* the man a picture of empty pockets. He gestured again.

I started toward the boat.

"Okay," Peter said, following me. "This river isn't very wide. We could always swim to shore."

We boarded, and took a pair of seats in the center under a cloth shade. Boxes and a small animal cage, from which came mewing sounds, lay in the stern. The man climbed into a seat up front with what Peter said was the steering apparatus, and did something we couldn't see.

A putt-putt noise started up and we moved away from the dock. This vessel was bigger than our little two person boats. Once we reached the middle of the river, the putt-putt stopped, and we floated with the current.

This was better than walking, and somehow I knew this is what we were supposed to do. I still didn't like being lead around like this, but couldn't figure out a way to do anything else. The sides of the river valley were lined with tall mountains. I sure didn't want to have to climb them.

"I guess they use the motor when they're going upstream," Peter said. "I wonder what they use for fuel."

"I wonder why he's doing this. He doesn't want anything from us," I said, watching a large white bird sailing across the sky.

"I'd say this is his duty, to transport people and goods up and down the river. I'd guess he offers anyone walking on the road a ride."

"But why?"

"Maybe some kind of levy or taxes for whoever rules this world," Peter said. "With that Gate, there's got to be a connection with the world we came from."

"If you say so." He was probably right. He and Papa.

A pang of homesickness hit me. "Mama," I whispered. If Peter heard me, he didn't say anything.

We sat back in the pleasant breeze and watched the world slide by. When it grew dark, the boatman pulled over to the bank and tied up.

Peter asked the boatman something I didn't catch, but the latter shook his head and moved away.

We ate our food and curled up in the cloak for the night.

#

In the morning, the boatman approached us and beckoned toward the boat. There wasn't much of a trail here, so we boarded. Again, he refused to talk to us.

"I wonder how much longer this trip will take," Peter said, fidgeting in his seat. "Can you ask him?"

I *sent* the boatman several different numbers of suns with question marks, but got no response.

Shortly after midday, another river joined ours from the right, making it much bigger and faster. The boatman struggled at times to keep us close to the left bank. Once we swung around wildly, and Peter grabbed me.

"Hang on, Perri," he yelped, clutching the rail with his other hand.

"Wow, what a ride," I said, after the boat was under control.

"Yeah. This river is too strong for this little boat. Are you okay?"

"Yes, you?"

"Maybe a couple bruises. Let's hope this doesn't happen again." We sat back and tried to relax.

Late in the day we passed behind a long island, and stopped for the night at the far end. We found a much used fire circle and padded sleeping area under wide trees waiting for us.

The boatman continued to evade us.

"I suspect he thinks we're a couple of the big shots," Peter said.

"Us?"

"Well, look. These people are all small and dark. I'm taller than any of them and there's our curly hair."

"Okay," I said, glancing at the boatman. Peter did have much broader shoulders than the locals had.

We continued on down the river, staying close to the left bank, stopping occasionally for breaks. Peter and I took advantage of this by stretching our legs, running around. We needed the exercise.

On the afternoon of the second day after that, we pulled up to a stone dock at the base of a mountain of a gray building. Several people in brown and yellow tunics stood nearby, watching us approach.

"This looks like a place for a Gate," I said, but I couldn't *sense* one. Peter and I debarked and followed a path of large, flat stones. I saw a village just upriver and well back from it, but only wild forest on the other side of the river.

My innards screamed for us to get out of here and go home, but my brain knew that we had to find a Gate to do that. Since I could not *sense* one here, all we could do was follow the route laid out for us.

The walkway led to several flights of stairs, partway around the building, and into a long archway. After the last turn, I could see the deep blue sea.

Inside the archway, a man in yellow indicated that we were to follow a narrow orange rug across a bare yellow room out into a large open place. In the center sat a small room with clear walls that shimmered.

A man in green stood nearby and waved us into it. When we stepped in, the room dropped into darkness. Peter said, "Hey," and grabbed at a bar along the side. I clutched at him. It felt like my stomach was going to come up out of my mouth.

When we stopped, the door opened to reveal a man in a yellow tunic and golden hair tumbling over his shoulders. Taller and much wider than Charley, he looked like a sun. Nodding at us, he gently took our arms and led us across to a normal-sized room with lots of brown seats and no windows. He ushered us in, backed out, and the door slid shut.

"Now what?" I demanded of the room. Neither of the two doors would open. Peter said they needed some kind of key. I paced the floor as Peter worked his way around the room, examining everything. Had we been led into a trap?

"Sit down and see what's out there," Peter said.

I plopped into a stuffed chair and *reached*. My Talent was back. There were not very many people compared to the building where I'd found Peter. And no sign of a Gate. There had to be a Gate, it was practically impossible to get back up to the one we'd come through. Maybe it was shut down for some reason. I tugged at a curl.

The door slid open and a young blond couple walked in. They opened the other door and beckoned to us. We followed, and saw a large tub of steaming water, a pile of cloths, and another of clothes on a table. A toilet sat in a side cubicle. The female waved her hand around and the male followed her out before I could let loose of a question.

Peter said, "How long has it been since we've taken a bath together?" He stripped off his tunic and tossed it into a corner. I laid my cloak on a chair. We sat on a bench and took our boots off. My toes wiggled blissfully.

"Room for two," Peter said, gazing at the tub. He jumped up, pulled down his pants, stepped into the tub and sat.

"Come on in, it's great."

I stripped off my tunic and pants, climbed in, and ducked under. It was heaven. The hot water pulled out all the little aches and pains. When I came up for air, I shook my head, splashing Peter. He splashed back. We splashed and laughed until we could hardly breathe.

"Remember when Mama would yell at us for splashing all the water out?" Peter grinned.

"Yes, and we had to clean it up after." We hugged mentally. "Here, have some soap." He tossed it at me. "Get those nice breasts clean. You're becoming quite a woman."

"I know." I pushed away a tendril of unease. Even though we'd been raised with the same lack of shame of the body and its products as the Bramites, still every once in a while Mama's Earth-learned feelings of privacy came through.

We soaped thoroughly, including our hair, and splashed some more. It was a wonderful break from all the stress we'd been under.

Finally Peter said, "I think it's time to get out, my sister, the prune."

I splashed, climbed out and wrapped a drying cloth around me. He followed. "Oh, Anne will be very happy with that," I smirked.

"You are positively glowing," Peter retorted, grabbing his own drying cloth.

"Yes, well," I glanced away. "I'm pregnant."

"You're what?" Peter dropped his cloth, picked it up, and sat down.

"You heard me. Charley couldn't wait. We put up mental blocks."

"Perri, you shouldn't be running around like this."

"It'll be a long time before it slows me down." I grabbed a tunic off the pile of clean clothes and slipped it on.

"Does Mama know?" He continued drying himself.

"Of course. I don't think she's too thrilled about being a grandmother so soon." We rubbed our hair dry, finished dressing, and wiped out our boots. I squeezed the slippers they'd left us into one of my pockets.

I heard a noise at the outer door. It let me open it. The couple stood there, smiling, and motioned for us to come out.

"Just a moment," I said, turning back to the room.

We gathered our things and followed them to a room down the hall full of machinery. They sat us in big chairs with things in the arms and back and around our heads that poked and prodded us. I tried to get up, but something held me down.

'I'm getting really tired of this,' I *sent* to Peter.

'What can we do? We can't even talk to these people.'

After that, we were shown to still another room. This one had a large bed, and a table with breads, bowls of soups and porridges, and cups of drinks. The female folded her hands under a cheek, and pointed to the bed. I nodded. The couple turned and left. Again, I couldn't get the door to open. The other one, to the sanitary room, stood wide.

"Not again," I grumbled. Peter was already stuffing his face. I did a quick check, the food seemed to be okay, so I joined him. As I was finishing, Peter prowled around the room.

"Same old, same old," he said, as he came back to me and yawned. I echoed it, and we crawled into bed. It was so soft and cozy, I barely had time to think that something was wrong timewise before Peter slid in beside me and I fell asleep.

Chapter 19   Cray and Gate

I woke up suddenly, sat up, and looked around. Peter was hunched over the table, eating. Before I could say anything, the outer door opened, and the male from the day before stood there beckoning. Peter jumped up, looked around, shook his head and pointed to me. The man continued to beckon, until Peter pushed him out the door and slammed it shut.

I climbed out of bed, grabbed my clothes, and ran into the other room. The outer door stayed closed.

When I came out, Peter went in, and I grabbed a bite to eat.

"Are you ready?" Peter asked, coming out of the other room.

"Yes." I collected my cloak and bag, and went to the door. It opened. The man was still standing there, beckoning. Peter, behind me, tried to pull me back, but the door shoved us out into the hall. Shrugging, we followed him through the halls and down the lift to a small room, where a lean, brown man sat behind a table.

He talked to us in what sounded to Peter like several different languages, none of which either of us understood. When we kept shaking our heads, the man took a small device out of a drawer and set it on the table in front of him. He spoke, touched a place on the thing, said something else.

The machine spoke in a sort of Standard. "Hello" I heard, through Peter as usual, a high and tinny voice.

"Hello," I said aloud, as Peter goggled. Nothing seemed strange to me anymore. The man said something else and touched the machine.

It said, "You go on boat to next river, then to new home."

"No," I said, shaking my head. "Do you have a Gate here? We have to get back to our home world."

The man's eyes widened as the machine spat out a stream of gibberish.

"No Gate. New village. Stay here two days for boat. Go." The man made a shooing motion.

As we left, I wondered whether it had been such a smart idea to mention the Gate.

The blond man escorted us back to the room with the bed. I tried to go down a side hall, but something invisible stopped me. Back in the room, Peter and I stared at each other.

"I'm not going to sit in this room for two days with not even a window to look out of." I kicked a small basket on the floor.

"So how are you going to get out?" Peter scanned the room.

I glared at him and plopped down into a soft red chair. Closing my eyes, I *reached* out. I could sense two people across the hall, and several in other rooms on this level. All I could tell was that they were aware, and basic emotions. I *found* four or five above us, and many people below. My Talent was finally back to normal. "I've found a lot of people, but no sign of a Gate,"

"Maybe there'll be one where we're going." Peter stared at a large picture on the wall opposite the door, beyond the bed. It showed grass in the foreground, with forest behind. He touched it at several places, but nothing happened. Then he ran his hand around the dark brown frame. When he reached the top right corner, the picture moved slightly to the left.

The tall tree at the left edge disappeared, and a strip at the right side became scrubby growth.

"Hey, watch this," Peter said. He touched it again. The forest moved right some more, showing a wider stretch of shrub. The next touch showed a strip of beach, and the one after it, a bit of blue sea. The forest was almost gone. Several more of the sea, until we came to one that showed the edge of a paved area.

Two more touches, and we saw people moving around a wide paved area with the sea beyond. "Hey, this is live," Peter said. "This is a window."

"How can a window show different scenes?"

"It's not like you can open it and stick your head out. There's some kind of device outside that shows different views and sends them in here to this screen. But at least we can see outside."

When the female brought the next meal, I asked if we could go outside, *projecting* a picture of us on grass. She stared at me blankly and left. The door snicked shut behind her.

"Nice try, Perri."

"Shut up."

84

Playing with the picture got boring after two days, but we had nothing else to do. I pulled out all our clothes, looking for something to mend. Mending was my least favorite task, but anything to keep busy.

Peter was in the sanitary room when I turned to a view straight up the riverbank. A tall thin man in greens and browns strode toward me. Someone new. I *reached*.

"What," Peter mumbled, coming out.

"Look. There's Cray, the alien I saw on Harmony."

"How do you know it's him? What's he doing here?"

"I just know. They sent him after us."

"Sending someone after us I get, but why him?"

"Because he's the only one who's actually seen me." I *touched* Cray. He stopped and looked up at the building. I *projected* a boat going down the river with us in it. He twitched, and disappeared below the window.

"He knows we're here," I said. "Now something will happen." I danced around the room. Peter joined me. After a while I *felt* Cray's presence nearby. He was with a few other people. We waited.

The young couple opened the door and beckoned. We grabbed our things and followed them, down and around to the open area with the little room that took us to a bigger area and a dock. Wider than our house, the blue and white boat tied up to it was larger than our meeting hall. It had a cabin on it as big as my home.

"Wow," Peter said, as we stopped and stared. Then I saw the endless sea beyond it. Were we going out on that?

I *felt* Cray nearby, but couldn't see him. We, and a few others who'd been waiting, boarded, and we found seats up front where we could see out. The blonde female buckled us into harnesses, and she and her mate sat behind us.

As the motor started up, I heard a thump and the boat rocked. I was sure Cray was now onboard with us, but the harness wouldn't let me turn to look.

The rocking of the boat was soothing, like lying on a tree branch in a light wind. We moved backward until the boatman could turn us around. Out past a line of rocks, we picked up speed and the boat rocked even more. I'd never seen waves this high on our sea. Someone behind me groaned.

When the sun dropped behind us, an older woman brought us food. I'd been about to start searching my cloak pockets. After we ate, she took us, one by one, to a tiny sanitary room at the back of the cabin. As I passed Cray, I nodded to him. He twitched his head in return.

As the light dimmed, the older woman showed us how to make the seats lean back. I laid my cloak over us. Every time I dozed off, a larger rocking would wake me up. Finally I slept, for Peter shook me awake.

In the morning, we received more food and another trip to the sanitary room. I watched the land go by. We kept fairly close to the wild and bushy shore, with groups of tall trees here and there. Occasionally, a stream would flow out into the sea, creating a small beach. Once, I saw a large, gray beast with horns on its head.

All this adventuring was interesting, even fun at times, but underneath I knew I not only had to get Peter and me back home, but find out more about how the Gates worked.

Peter slept a lot, until he woke me from a doze. "Hey, look." He pointed. We were approaching a light grey building even larger than the one we'd left. It hunched on the corner of land where another river met the sea.

The boat slowed, and docked at a much larger landing area. Two other boats, one like ours and one smaller, rocked at the dock. A crowd of people milled around. Presently we were allowed to disembark, and found Cray waiting for us.

"This is my twin brother, Peter," I said to Cray, *showing* him us together as babies. A man with a red badge said something to Cray. He led the three of us into the building and up in a lift to a long room lined with shelves.

We sat in rough wooden chairs at a large worktable scattered with papers, brown boxes, and odds and ends. One of the two men in green, with dark, narrow faces sitting across from us, spoke to Cray. They also looked at Peter and me from time to time. Peter *sent* to me that they sounded stern, and that Cray was pleading his case. I sat there in my silence and watched their faces.

Presently the men rose and left. Cray put his hands on our shoulders, keeping us seated.

"What's going on?" I asked.

Cray shrugged.

In a moment another person entered, clad in a shiny brown suit that covered all but the reflective mask over the face. Even though I couldn't access the person, I somehow knew he/she was a gatekeeper. He said something to Cray, who flinched. The person turned and left. Cray indicated that we were to follow.

We proceeded along grey corridors and down a lift to a place with a heavy silvery door. Both the gatekeeper and a guard there had to put their hands on a dark patch on the wall before the door would open. Following the gatekeeper down a passage through a forest of machines humming to themselves, Peter *sent*, 'Uncle Art would love this.'

I felt the Gate very close, and tucked away my Talents as best I could. In an open area we found a little white house with a stand by the door. The latter had a lot of little buttons, one big knob, and a small screen with changing pictures.

While Cray worked with the buttons, I *sensed* Peter following him with his mind.

'Peter, no,' I *cried*. He ignored me. The door opened.

Cray ushered us inside, and followed. We sat in hollowed out cushions that wrapped themselves around us. Cray *sent* reassurance. It seemed too easy, that our path and these people we couldn't understand would just lead us to a Gate and send us home. I shivered.

I *shared* with Peter what I saw outside.

'Probably select a world with a button and start it going with the big one,' he *sent*.

'But there's nothing like that at our Gate.'

The room went dark, and I felt the misty ooziness of the Gate. The room jittered for a moment, then became still. Peter laid his hand on my arm. A faint, sweetish aroma touched my nose, and suddenly I couldn't breathe.

After a long moment, the door opened.

Chapter 20   Island World

As the cushions let us out, I said, "We're still here."

Cray cocked his head, frowned, and trotted to the door. He swung it open and said, "No, it cannot be."

I peered around him and saw green jungle and blue ocean.

"This isn't Harmony," I added as Cray stepped out onto the yellow porch. Peter pushed up beside me.

"Not Onan." Cray looked from side to side. He *sent* me a picture of a green cone on a flat blue surface.

"So where are we?" Peter asked.

Cray shrugged and turned back to the door. I looked around and saw only a blank yellow wall.

"What do we do now?" I asked. *Not again. Not another world to hike across.* My heart sunk to my knees.

Cray stepped off the porch and pointed to the path leading down into the jungle. "Come," he said.

Peter grabbed my hand as we followed him. The sun, though still low, was hot. It was cooler in the jungle, but very damp. The trees were full of noisy critters, from high, squeaky ones, to midlevel growlers, but I didn't actually see any.

Long vines studded with huge pink flowers hung from branches. The trees looped about each other like a loose ball of yarn, with the vines weaving them together. A sweetish, marshy smell hung about us.

The path was wide enough for two, and although the trees grew together overhead, there was plenty of clear space above us. Cray had found a stick and was thrashing about with it on either side.

"To scare away dangerous critters, Perri," Peter said, reading the question in my mind.

I walked in a cloud of gloom. I was tired of walking all over strange worlds, I was tired of not being able to understand anyone except Peter. I was tired, period.

My pregnancy wasn't affecting me yet, but I knew I had to get home while I could still walk easily. I remembered how the other women waddled around near the end of their pregnancies.

At least I was with Peter. Even as annoying as he could be, I thanked the Oneness that we were together. But I missed Mama and Papa and Charley. When would I ever see them again? I bit my lip to keep back the tears.

Sometime later we came to an open spot, where several trees had been struck down, trunks and stumps sharp black points. "Looks like a lightning strike," Peter said, as I collapsed to the ground.

We sat and ate a bit; Cray still had food. He *showed* me a tall green cone linked by a line through several islets to a large island with a Gate on it.

"Okay," I said, nodding.

As we continued on, the path was not as steep, but there were more buzzy insects. They seem to like the men better than me; both Peter and Cray were continually swatting at them.

The sun was low to our right beneath a layer of dark clouds as we reached an open area leading down to the sea. The path curved around to our left. A nearby stream trickled out to the ocean.

Cray set his bundle down near the edge of the trees just as a clap of thunder made me jump. Before I could say anything, the heavens opened and we were soaked. We huddled under a tree until the storm passed. The sun was still above the horizon.

Peter trotted down to the sea, bent over and put a hand in. "It's warm," he said, returning to us. He stripped and ran back into the water. When it reached his waist, a long way out, he turned and yelled, "Come on in."

I looked at Cray. He rose and walked down the beach from us. I watched as he disrobed and walked into the water. Slipping out of my clothes, I followed Peter.

We had a great time splashing around as the sun set. It was wonderful to feel clean again. When we came out, our clothes were nearly dry. After we dressed, we waited for Cray to come back to us. He was smiling.

We camped there, on the soft sand below the grass. Best sleep I'd had for a while.

In the morning, we headed down the path, through thick bushes, around the base of the hill and into the rising sun. After a few minutes of squinting and trying to see where we were going, Peter stopped.

"I have an idea," he said. He cut a few very large leaves off a low bush, some pieces of vine, tied the vine through holes in the leaves to make us hats.

"Your bonnet, Perri," he said, handing me one.

"Thanks." I turned it in my hands and put it on my head. By angling it so the long part stuck out in front, I could keep the sun out of my eyes.

Cray beamed approval as the men donned theirs. We continued on. As we climbed up a small hill, I saw a series of islands stringing off in the distance.

I *reached*. Although there was no one else on this island, I could *sense* others on the next few islands. I could not *sense* a Gate, though.

Continuing on around, we came to another ridge. When we climbed it, I saw that the path led out to the end of the land. It was bare and rocky here.

"What is this?" I asked. Cray *showed* me a line between this island and the next, which didn't look that far away. As we neared the end of the ridge far out into the sea, I saw two stout poles, one on each side of the path.

Then I saw the bridge. A rope bridge was suspended between the two poles and two others on the island across the way.

Cray *sent* me a picture of people braiding vines together.

"Hey, cool," Peter said, shaking the bridge.

"Stop," Cray bellowed. He *showed* both of us how a swinging bridge would break.

Peter backed off.

"I'm not going on that thing," I said, shivering.

"That's where the path goes," Peter said, taking a step onto the bridge. Cray gently pushed me forward onto it, as Peter danced away, sending the bridge swinging.

I yelped and grabbed the rails.

"Stop," Cray yelled, and put his hands on my shoulders, preventing me from backing up.

Cray yelled at Peter again. Peter stopped, and walked more sedately. Cray and I started forward.

I grimly clutched the side rails, stared straight ahead, and put one foot after the other. *At least there's water down there, not rocks. But how deep is it?*

It seemed longer than the trail on Harmony from top to beach, but eventually we made it across. I turned back and looked at the island we'd come from. The tall green cone looked taller than what I expected from our descent.

Cray took my arm and turned me to face forward. We followed the path on this island. A quarter of the way around we came to a village. Round huts with thatched roofs circled an open area containing a large fire pit surrounded by wide stone benches.

Small brown people rushed out of the huts and gathered around us, jabbering away.

Cray held his hands up. The people quieted down. He spoke to them, but I couldn't understand it. Nor could Peter. A man with white hair and taller than most, led us to a wide bench on one side of the fire pit. We sat.

A woman wearing a skirt of colorful leaves, and purple flowers in her hair brought us roundish orange fruits. Peter grabbed one and bit into it before I could say anything.

"Mmm," he said around the mouthful of orange pulp. I checked and found no danger, so I took one and bit into it. The fruit was sweet with a marvelous tang to it. We each ate two while Cray munched on a large one.

"Who are these people?" I finally asked. All I could sense from them was a feeling of contentment.

Cray shrugged.

Several men busied about building a fire, and a group of young people arrived carrying several small dead animals. After the women prepared the critters, the men roasted the meat over the fire. The first woman offered us each a small piece.

I sensed no problem with the meat, so we took ours. It was mild and sweet. There were also some orange root vegetables.

After supper, the people sang and told tales. Cray chuckled occasionally so we did too, even though we had no idea what our hosts were saying.

Then Cray began talking, in a story telling mode. We caught a few words here and there, but I wasn't satisfied with that.

We need to learn his language, I thought. I couldn't stand not knowing what they were saying.

Finally we were allowed to retire to a sleeping place. I prayed to the Oneness to help us get to a Gate soon.

#

In the morning, the little brown people fed us more fruit and urged us to stay.

Cray shook his head, said something I didn't understand, and led us on down the trail.

On the far side of this island we came to a place with a few shacks and a dock. A small blue boat bobbed beside the pier. In the distance I saw more islands. I heaved a sigh of relief when I realized that I didn't have to cross another rope bridge.

As we approached the buildings, a man tall and thin like Cray came out, and they spoke. I saw the man nod, which I took as a hopeful sign. They turned and beckoned to Peter and me.

We all boarded the boat. This one had no shade, so we held on to our hats. The craft didn't go very fast and it took most of the day to get to the next island. This islet was much smaller than the others, and only had one low hill.

At the dock there, with its own shacks, a man awaited. The three of them talked while I fumed because we couldn't understand them. The two men went into a shack and Cray turned to us.

He *showed* me a picture of a green circle with little boats and stick figures on either side, with a line straight across, and a little circle in the center.

"Okay," I said, nodding my head. "There's another boat on the other side," I told Peter.

We took off up the hill, and at the top found a copse of trees and a spring. It was a pleasant place to camp. I looked back and could see the top of the green cone beyond the in between island.

Peter peered at the spring. "Why a spring up here?" he muttered. He touched something. "Oh, I see. It's artificial, for travelers."

I turned back toward the direction we were headed. Down below, I saw shacks and a dock, but no boat. There were more islands in a row, and one very tall mountain in the far distance. I *reached*, found people, but no sign of a Gate.

We settled down for the night. The air cooled off after sunset, when breezes swept the area. Peter and I cuddled together to keep warm. I prayed for there to be a boat in the morning.

#

When I awoke, the sea around the dock was empty. My heart sank, and I looked farther out. Something floated on the water near the next island. I hoped it was a boat. As we descended, as the trail wound around between hillocks and among boulders, I watched as the object on the water approached our island. It was a boat.

We stood in the shade of a large tree overhanging the shacks and waited for the craft to arrive. When the boat docked, Cray led us around to where two men were talking in front of one of the shacks.

They greeted us, more talk, and we boarded the boat, which was just like the one we'd ridden to this island the previous day. There were more swells here, and I saw a large grey fish jump out of the water and splash back down.

We passed the first island and the next two, tiny things no bigger than River Point, and landed at a much wider place. Here there were two large buildings and several smaller ones.

Chapter 21   Last Island and Gate

Quite a few people milled about, watching our boat arrive. While most of them were like Cray, there were a few of the little brown people. Others my height were very pale and wore red fronds in their reddish blond hair. Everyone wore simple clothes in browns, tans, and greens.

A large man all in green, with a pair of broad blue strips of cloth hanging down from his shoulders, approached and said something to Cray while looking me over.

I heard Cray mention 'Gate'.

The large man led us through the crowd to a yellow building. Inside, we sat at a table and he brought food, a sort of stew with meat in it. Peter gobbled it down, but I just picked at my food. I was too anxious to eat much.

After the meal, Cray led us to doors at the side of the room that opened into smaller rooms with narrow beds. "Sleep here," he said, and somehow I knew what he meant.

The bed was barely comfortable, but I fell asleep almost immediately.

When I awoke, it took me a moment to remember where I was. *How many more nights was I going to have to spend on this world before I get home to Harmony?*

We were given breakfast, provisions, and directions. Cray led Peter and me to the main road, which was wide enough for four people to walk side by side easily, and very flat and smooth. A tall man trotted past us, pulling a small brown cart with a gray cloth covering it.

"That's why the road is so wide," Peter said.

I wished I could ride in a cart for a while. We passed little reddish houses here and there among the wide trees along the way.

The road turned inland and uphill. A low slope at first, but it soon became steeper.

When we reached the top of the hill, and I saw higher mountains in the distance, I groaned.

"Why can't we go around?" I asked, swinging my arm.

Cray *showed* me a long narrow island, with a string of mountains down the long axis. There was a line across the narrow axis, where we were, with boats at each end. Then a line around the long end, followed by a row of five suns, appeared.

"Okay, I said. *Please, Oneness, get us somewhere soon.*

The road went along the hill around the valley and up again, in switchbacks and level stretches.

"Yeah, it would be too hard to pull carts up a too steep a road," Peter said. Up ahead, we saw the man and cart still bouncing along. "I guess he does it for a living."

We plodded upward. It was a little cooler on this island. Tiny purple flowers spread in masses on either side of the road. Scattered, twisted trees sprinkled the hills, with low gray growth in between.

Near the top, we came to a huge oval valley. A side road led down into it where a town was laid out. Across the main road was a place with benches under a roof, and in the rear, a long stretch of covered sleeping spaces. Trees in back hid a latrine.

"Can we stop for a bit?" I asked, eyeing the sleeping spaces.

"Yes," Cray said. The sun hung low in the west. "We camp here," he added, waving his arm.

I headed back to the sleeping area, chose a thick mattress, and lay down. It felt so good, but still not as comfortable as my bed at home.

#

In the morning, Peter shook me awake. "Come on, Perri, we need to get going." He helped me up.

The road stayed level for a while, and started down the other side. I could see the islands in the distance. The tall one looked closer, but I still couldn't *sense* a Gate.

The way took us between two rocky hills. Cray, in front, suddenly stopped.

"Holey Moley," Peter said, peering over his shoulder.

"Why did we stop?" I asked, trying to see between them. Cray moved back.

The road ended in a drop into a wide pit that stretched far to our left.

"Oh, no," I wailed. This was too much.

"Oh yes," Peter said. "We'll have to find a way around it. Perhaps on the other side of this hill." He gestured to the right.

"Yes," Cray said.

We went back to the beginning of the hill and looked for a way around it. A path led off to the right. Peter and I followed Cray along the way. I wondered how long that pit had been there.

The path was narrow, and we had to walk in single file. It wound between boulders, scattered trees, and piles of rocks. I was glad I'd had a good night's rest.

At a large, empty area that dipped in the center like a bowl, Peter said, "Let's go around." I felt something wrong with the area, too, but Cray started across.

A grumble, a crack, and the ground fell out from under him. Cray disappeared into the hole.

"No," I yelped.

"Stay here," Peter said. He dropped to his hands and knees and crawled out to the opening.

"Peter," I cried.

"He's okay. We just have to figure out how to get him up." Peter leaned forward and the edge crumbled. He scrabbled backward. He turned and looked at me. "Do you have anything like a rope?"

"I don't know. Let me look. Uncle Art gave me a bunch of stuff." I pawed through my cloak pockets and bags. "Oh, here, will this work?" I tossed him a roll of fine cord. "Uncle Art said it's a lot stronger than it looks. Something from the ship."

Peter unrolled the cord and pulled on it. "Feels tough." He tied one end around a rock and tossed the other end down into the hole. I watched as he leaned back against the boulder and pulled.

After a short time, he stopped and let the cord sag. "Can I help?" I asked, moving toward him.

"No. Stay back. I don't want to have to worry about you, too," he panted. He shook the line a little, then leaned back and pulled.

After a few more sessions, and a few more pieces of the edge of the hole broke off, Cray's head appeared above the side. His hands reached out to pull himself up, the ground disappeared and so did he.

"Please, Oneness, help us get him out," I prayed as I *lifted* him. Cray's head appeared, he rose, and fell on the solid ground, gasping.

"Are you all right?" I heard Peter ask Cray, as I collapsed beside them.

"Yes." He did not open his eyes.

I felt a hand on my shoulder. "Perri?" Peter asked. "Did you…"

I barely moved my head. I had done it again, but this time I had consciously thought about lifting him for a brief second. If I could control it… Teleportation was a handy Talent, but why did it take so much out of me?

When I woke, the sun hovered low behind us. Cray was sitting up, clutching his knees, a large bandage on one arm.

Peter, pacing around, turned and plopped himself down beside me. "How are you doing?" he asked.

I shook my head, pushing myself up. "I can't go very far today."

"Well, there's no place any better to camp around here. I guess we missed the boat."

"Oh," I said, heart sinking. *Another day lost.* "Cray," I added.

Cray looked at me. I *sensed* a feeling of despair, and closed my eyes briefly.

"Will they come looking for us?" I asked, *sending* a picture of stick figures leaving the shacks and heading up the trail.

Cray shrugged and rolled over.

"You need to rest, Perri," Peter said, digging out the water jug. "Here, drink."

I took the jug and drank. Feeling better, I tried to get up. My body told me it wasn't going anywhere, so I lay down.

#

When Peter shook me awake, it was dark, with a dim line of light to the east. "Time to go," he said. "I scouted the way ahead yesterday, and it looks pretty easy."

"Oh," I muttered, sitting up. Cray stood staring into the dimness. Peter helped me to my feet, and we gathered my things.

"Come," Cray said. We continued along the path, nearly invisible in the darkness, Peter leading the way. As the day grew lighter and we curved back to the main road, we stepped up our pace.

On this side of the mountain, the hillsides were bare of plants except for a few little wispy things. As we plodded along, I thought, I've got to do something about this Gate business. After using my Talent to save Cray, I knew I could learn to control it. Surely there was a way I could use it to control the Gates, to protect our people.

Ignoring the barren landscape around me, I pondered on how this could be done. I would need Peter's help. Yes, he'd seen inside the controls.

I *asked* Peter what exactly had he seen when Cray operated the controls at the last Gate.

Peter glanced at me. 'All I saw was the control system, five rows of six buttons and two blue pads. There was nothing to identify which world a button would send us to.' He sighed. 'Below that was a blankness I couldn't penetrate.'

'So how did Cray know which button to push? What exactly did he do.?'

Peter stopped and closed his eyes. "He touched the left hand pad, and the button at the left end of the second row," he said aloud, and opened his eyes. "So the one on the left end of the top row must be for his home world. I moved his hand down." Peter smirked.

"Okay," I said, glancing at Cray's back ahead of us. "But how can we tell which one is for Harmony?"

"I don't know. Come on." We hurried to catch up with Cray.

We reached a grassy bank well above the sea. I stopped, looked at the farther islands, and *reached*. Several people moved around at the dock below, and there were more beings on the next two islands. On the third and final island, with the tall mountain, I *sensed* a Gate.

"Whew," I sighed. I had found the Gate. Now I wondered, how long would it take us to get there? The gloom began to thin out.

We moved on. The trail curved to the left and took us down to a settlement.

'I sensed the Gate,' I *told* Peter. He grinned.

The trail led us through the settlement of mud houses and past a pair of wooden shacks to the dock. This was twice as wide as the previous one, and much longer. Two boats bobbed alongside. One was like the ones we'd ridden in before, but the other was twice as big, with a cabin.

I hoped we'd be taking that one.

A man in green wearing some kind of official badge stopped us and talked to Cray. He asked something, and Cray shook his head. The other pointed back the way we'd come.

"No," I cried. Cray and the official looked at me. I pointed to the larger boat. The official shook his head. I grabbed Peter's hand and started toward the boat.

Cray stopped me with his hand. He *showed* me a picture of a card with writing on it, then shrunk it and *showed* it on the other side of the mountain.

"No," I cried again. We couldn't go all the way back just to get a card for the boat. That would take four more days. Trying to hold the tears back, I *showed* Peter what Cray had *sent* me.

Peter held up his hand, and tore off a small piece of his tunic. Closing his eyes, he crushed the bit of fabric in his hand.

I wondered what he was doing, but dared not *touch* him.

Peter opened his hand, displaying a perfect copy of what Cray had *shown* us. Cray took it, examined it, and handed it to the official.

He looked at it, at Peter, then at Cray. Finally, he nodded and led us to the large boat.

"How did you do that?" I demanded.

Peter grinned. "I have my Talents and you have yours."

We boarded and found seats by a window. The island we were leaving stretched away to my right as far as I could see, just like Cray's picture.

Other people settled in, an announcement blared, and we started out. As we pulled away from the dock, I saw the other end of the island stretching far in the distance in the opposite direction.

The boat sped south of the next island, bouncing from crest to crest. I hung on to the rail under the window and Peter hung on to me. I didn't hear any groans, so I guessed the other people were used to going this fast.

We thankfully came to a stop at the following island. Cray held us from getting off. The final island loomed large, and I definitely *sensed* a Gate on it. After a few people disembarked, and some others boarded, the boat took off again.

This time we didn't go as fast, and I was able to keep my eyes open and look around. A few more of those big gray fish jumped out of the water and splashed back down. A long bank of fluffy white clouds moved past us to the south. I inhaled great gulps of sea air.

As we approached, the mountain on the last island loomed over us. Behind the wide dock was a huge open plaza with little tents around the edges. Many people moved along the tents, and more stood behind a barrier at the back end of the dock.

Beyond the plaza, streets of green buildings streamed up the hillside. A few tall tan building poked up out of the mass of green.

I *reached* for the Gate. It was deep inside the mountain, at a level slightly lower than the plaza.

We followed the others off of the boat, and along a fence at the side of the dock. At the inland end of the dock, we were led into a fenced off walkway through the plaza. It curved to the right side of the town, to a small, square gray building against the mountain.

Inside a brown room, we stood at a counter and another man in green with a badge asked Cray some questions. After that, still another official led us down a long corridor.

"How," I began.

"We are going back into the mountain," Peter interrupted. As usual, he knew what I was going to say.

We turned right, went up a set of stairs, and turned again. I was lost, but I knew Peter could find his way out. After several more turns and another staircase, we were led into a large, blue room.

The far end was set up like a bedroom, and the front part like a meeting room. A long, brown table surrounded by chairs sat near a row of cabinets. We were ushered into seats along the side.

The official spoke to Cray, asking him questions. When Cray answered, I heard, via Peter, as usual, our names and 'gate'.

Was he going to let us through? Please, I thought, we need to get home.

After a few more words, he rose, and Cray followed, beckoning for us to come. The three of us followed the official in green down a brightly lit gray hallway to a massive door.

'Peter, when he goes into the controls, go with him but don't touch anything,' I *said*. 'I will go with you. We need to figure out how the Gates work.'

He nodded.

Inside, we were escorted to a small room to wait for our turn. The walls were somewhere between gray and brown, with built in seats, and a large screen on the back wall. This showed natural scenery and people playing various kinds of games.

"How long do we have to wait?" I asked. Cray shrugged.

Peter prowled the room and found a door into a sanitary room. When the door was closed, it matched the wall.

A female in light brown poked her head in and said something to Cray.

"Soon," he told us after she left.

I sure hoped so. I was more than ready to go and couldn't sit still. After all this, were we finally going to get back to Harmony?

Very shortly the door opened, and the official beckoned. We followed him down a white corridor to a large room full of machinery, with a round hut wearing a thatched roof in the center.

As we approached, I saw the stand with the screen and the buttons. I grabbed Peter's hand. We stopped behind Cray as he stood in front of the stand.

Peter and I linked and went into Cray's mind. We *asked*, and found that the button for Harmony was three across and three down. Cray didn't know much more about how the controls operated, just how to activate the Gate.

Cray touched the button for his world and I *jerked out*, crying out 'no' in my head. He did not seem to notice.

Cray led us into the hut, to the cushion seats.

'At least we'll be on a world we know, and know how to get back to Harmony,' Peter *sent* as the room went dark.

Chapter 22   Onan

As the cushions let us out in the white walled house, I was hit by a spasm of nausea.

Cray cocked his head and twitched it. 'Home. Onan,' he said.

"No, we need to go to Harmony," I cried.

"It's all right, Perri, we'll get there." Peter patted my shoulder.

We left the little house, and outside, I could see that the space around the house was smaller, and there seemed to be even more machines.

Cray spoke into a grill on the side of the stand. It squawked briefly, and Cray said something else.

We waited. I clenched my fist and chewed on it.

Presently a tall man in blues and greens appeared. "Cray," he said, added something else, and looked at Peter and me.

"OM Dree," Cray said, and we heard our names. Cray took my arm, Dree took Peter's, and they led us around the little house to a lift. It took us up to a bright square room, with a high ceiling. We all sat in a group of comfortable brown and green chairs.

Dree began to talk to Peter and me.

After a moment I said, "We can't understand what you're saying."

Dree looked at me, then at Cray, who said something. Dree gave Cray instructions. Cray twitched, rose, and took Peter and me to another room. This was another bedroom suite with a fake window in the back wall.

In my mind, Cray *sent* me a picture of me in faded red and him in brown, mouths open, with lines from each mouth to the other's ear, with slashes across them. Then the slashes melted away.

"Yes, yes, yes," I said, nodding.

He pointed to a table piled with dishes and foods, and said "tabr". We repeated it, and went on to chair, plate, and cup. Then Cray sat, said a word, and motioned us to sit. As we ate, he gave us names of things in his language, plus 'to eat', and 'to drink'.

After our meal, he went to another table with drawers and pulled out a thin book. In it we found lists of pictures and words. He went over the letters and pronunciation with us. When he left, he *let me know* he would be back after next sunrise.

Even though I was still anxious to get home, I was pleased to have a chance to learn their language. I'd gotten too used to my Talent, knowing what everyone was saying.

We studied the book until we couldn't stand it anymore and went to bed.

Next morning Cray appeared with our breakfast. After we ate, we worked with the book and using general conversation. It seemed easy to me, but Peter struggled. By the end of the day I was able to communicate adequately with Cray in his language. He told us not to let anyone know of our mind link. I had already suspected he wanted that kept secret.

After he left, we played with the window, looking at whatever it showed us. But we were still in prison. I yelled at Peter, threw things, and cried. He was patient with me, and I had a feeling he was enjoying this adventure a lot more than I was.

Day after day Cray brought breakfast and we studied his language, and day after day I asked when we could go home. Later, I asked to just to go outside. He always said not yet. We tried all different ways to get out the door, but even jumping on his back, I slipped off when he strode through the doorway.

The next day, he began teaching us things that I didn't think his bosses wanted us to know. Things like how the gatekeeper system worked.

The Gatekeepers' home world was at the center of a massive complex. In each of the six major directions from the globe of stars was a world they had colonized, key worlds. Each key world had a secondary world in each of the remaining five directions. Each secondary world had its own group of worlds. Onan was a secondary world and Harmony was in one of its groups.

Every day I pleaded and begged for him to let us out of that room. And almost every day I felt nauseous at times.

"I cannot. It is not allowed." I felt that he would if he could. He *sent* me a picture of the three of us each in a separate tiny room with no door or window, as he left.

I threw the book across the room. "It's not fair," I cried, stomping around. "I've got to get out of here."

"I'm with you," Peter said. "These walls are boring." He wandered around, poking into everything. At the back of a drawer he found a small box of sticks with colored ends. "Hey, look." I watched him as he took a green one and touched it to the white wall in a corner. A green dot appeared on the wall.

"Cool," he said. He drew a short line, then swooping lines all along the wall.

"Peter, are you sure you should be doing that?" He ignored me and drew leaves along the line. Well, I thought, they wouldn't have left the color sticks here if they didn't want us to use them. I picked out a red one and drew flowers along his line. He drew blue waves on another wall.

The blonde female said nothing about our artwork when she brought our supper. Later, surveying our work, I pointed out a black spot high up on a blue sky wall. Peter whipped out the blue stick and dabbed on it, but it wouldn't stay. I snipped off a bit of white from the coverlet, and he stuck it up there and dabbed over it.

"Perfect," he said. "You know what that is, don't you, Perri?"

"No, what?"

"A spy hole where someone on the other side can look through and watch us."

"What?" I clenched my fists and looked around. "Are there any more?"

"I don't think so." He spent some time looking, but didn't find any. "I'm ready for bed."

\#

In the morning, Cray approved our creation. He glanced up at the spy hole, and I *felt* him chuckle when he saw it colored over.

Days and tens of days passed. I could feel my baby growing inside me, and sometimes I was sick to my stomach in the morning and nauseated most of the day.

No matter how much I pestered him, I couldn't get anything out of Cray about how long we were going to be here, and why the gatekeepers wanted us to know his language.

I was beginning to forget what Papa looked like. Mama I saw every day in the mirror. I wondered what was going on back on Harmony, how they and Charley were coping without us, whether Peter and I would ever get back there.

Chapter 23   River Point

LYN

"You have to eat, babe," Larry said.

"I don't feel like it." I pushed the food around on my plate. "I want my children back."

"I know, but there's nothing we can do about it." He put a bite on a fork and held it out to me. I turned my head away.

Larry ate the bite and put the fork down. "Are we going to have to force feed you?" he asked, smiling at me.

"Maybe we should go after them," I said.

"What if they come back while we're gone? Anyway, there's no assurance that if we did go, that we'd go to the place where they are. Besides, we're too important here to go off for an unknown length of time." He took my hand. "They'll be back. Perri will find Peter and bring him home. They're survivors."

I sighed and squeezed his hand. "I suppose you're right."

Larry looked out the window. "Time for the council meeting. Put that away and let's go."

#

As the high council assembled on the stage of the meeting hall, I automatically *reached* for Perri and Peter. The emptiness of their absence overwhelmed me, and I sat down. I told myself that they were alive and well on another world, and that they'd be back. *Before the baby comes.*

"The council," I said aloud, focusing on the people around me. Bay and Pauli sat on one green couch, Art and Betty on the other. Larry sprawled in a blue chair in a corner, and Adam took the red chair. These stuffed seats had been recovered from our lounge on the Emprisa, the ship that brought us to Harmony.

Emek marched in, trailed by his mate, Sanga, Noa, Karil, Treesa, and several other Bramite women her age.

"What's this?" Larry drawled.

I knew what they wanted, but didn't say anything.

"They have a request to put before the council," Emek said, as Sanga opened her mouth. "It will be heard, but first, Noa."

Noa, just about to sit down, remained standing. Edges of her wide eyes curled around the side of her face.

"Council members and guests," she began. "We have a major problem at North Point. Several couples, including two pregnant women, went up there without proper supplies or personnel. One of the women died from complications of childbirth, because there were no medics with them. The baby was brought down here; he is in critical condition after two days with no food. We are doing our best to save him."

"My suggestion is that we bring those people down here and plan properly for the settlement. We could make sure that they have all the skilled personnel they need, and all the supplies required. We don't want to lose any more of our young women." She sat down.

"Yes," Sanga cried. "We need them down here."

Emek glared at her.

"Not just yet," Adam said, glancing at Emek, who nodded. "We need to discuss our water problem. I went up to check on the mill this morning, and there was barely enough water flow to keep it moving. The wells are barely sufficient for drinking and cooking. We need the river water for washing and crops. Rain has been scarce the last few years. We can't afford to bring more people back down here."

"What about the other pregnant woman?" I asked. "You can't just leave her up there with no medical support."

"I have a pair of newly trained medics we can send up," Noa said. As the head medic, she was in charge of teaching young women the art of healing.

"Good," Emek said. "Who else do we need to send?"

"A crop overseer and a warehouse manager," Noa replied. "I talked to Ned, who brought the baby down."

"Good," Adam said. "Under the circumstances, we might as well get North Point set up right. I know, Lyn," as I opened my mouth. "We also need a pair with Talent, so we can keep in touch."

"Who isn't pregnant." I put my two cents in.

"Okay." Adam grinned. "For now, we'll send Allen up with Gabe, the medics and maybe a few others."

"Meanwhile, Larry, Art and his son, and Bay can get together to come up with some ideas about our water situation."

"What about our children?" Treesa demanded.

"They will have to stay up there for the time being. If you want to go up and see them, you're welcome to go along. Let me know, so I can rearrange work schedules." Adam looked around. "Anything else?"

"Just get the word out to everyone to be very careful using water," I said. Two fewer mouths—the thought came unbidden—and the emptiness came howling back. The rest of the Four, Adam, Bay and Pauli, gathered me in and held me close. I felt Adam's pain as well as mine.

Chapter 24   Learning a Language

Cray showed us how to clear part or all of a wall, so we could make new art. Peter was much better at it than I was. On the two side walls we painted trees, and only changed minor things like flowers. We made a beach scene with trees at the edges on the wall with the outside door. The back wall, with 'window' and door to sanitary room, we played with, drawing new scenes every day.

The artwork helped us get through the days, but not enough. We were still trapped in one room. I'd tried *reaching* several times, but Cray was the only one whose mind I could connect with. We had good food, clean clothes, games on the screen and the artwork with which to entertain ourselves and exercise our minds. Peter and I did a set of physical exercises every day to keep our bodies in shape.

But I couldn't get rid of a scared feeling in my gut. The pressure to leave and get us home only grew, and I began to worry about my baby. She appeared to be fine, but I wondered whether she was getting the proper nutrients and what would happen if I was still here when my time came. For the first time I really thought about giving birth and caring for a baby. To be responsible all day, all night, every day for this new little being. More than ever, I wanted to be home with Mama when this happened.

Also, I kept wondering why they wanted to teach us their language. To communicate, yes, but why? Did they do this with all the natives on the worlds they took over? I asked Cray, and he said they would pick a few at first, and they'd teach others of a select group. Most of the people on this world did not know the gatekeeper language.

"I thought they wanted us off our world," Peter said.

"I don't know what they want," Cray replied.

A few days later, Dree came in with Cray. "Very good," he said, looking at the walls. "Sit." We all sat around the table. Dree talked to us, testing our knowledge of his language.

Even though he had no mind link receptors that I could find, I could *sense* what he was thinking.

He wanted us back on our world, even though the gatekeepers didn't. I *probed* him as much as I dared while Peter was talking. Suddenly Dree grabbed his head. Oops, I thought, and quickly *backed out*.

"Head pain," Dree said, rising. Cray looked at me. I looked down at my hands. "Enough for today," Dree said, and left.

"What did you do?" Peter asked. He knew me too well.

"He get head pain often," Cray said.

Later, I considered the information I'd got from Dree. This was one of many Gatekeeper worlds. They ran the world, using natives like Cray and Dree as links to their people. Dree was a direct link. He protected his people as much as possible while doing what Gatekeepers wanted.

#

Six days later, Dree returned. This time he asked questions about our world. I signaled to Peter to let me talk, and not to volunteer anything.

"How many of you on that world?" Dree asked.

"Lots," I said. "I don't know a number." I looked at Peter. "Do you have any idea?"

He shrugged. "Maybe six hundred or so."

"Still small (a word I didn't know)", Cray said. "Tell me about what you eat."

"We grow grains, vegetables, fruits, and collect nuts and fruits from the forest. Also fish from the sea. If we get good rains, we have good crops, and a lot to eat. If not, then not so much."

He continued to question me about our settlement and the people in it. I gave away as little information as I could. Once he asked about the brown creatures, and I took it to mean the twitterers. And then I *saw* in his mind he meant the Wati, but he didn't correct me. What was he up to? I knew he must be recording this somehow, to take to the Gatekeepers.

As he left, I followed him in my mind. He went up to the highest level of the building that I could penetrate and met someone I couldn't place, or *sense* anything about that person. They talked for a moment, and parted. Dree came down several levels and the other just disappeared.

Cray said, "You did well." He gave us our lesson for the day, and departed.

"I wonder why he didn't ask about the Wati." I said.

"I don't know. He didn't sound entirely happy with these other guys running his world."

"True. Let's eat."

"You're always hungry," Peter said as I went to the food coldbox.

"I'm eating for two, remember."

"And you heave up half of it in the mornings." He followed me over.

"Oh shut up." I grabbed a red fruit and stalked to my chair.

#

The next morning, I felt an uneasiness within me. The baby seemed a little off. I had a sudden craving for a particular fruit, and ate the last two. The uneasiness faded away, and I kept it down.

I *touched* my baby and felt a want for something that was in that fruit. Oh, no, I thought, butterflies in my belly. *I'm not getting the right nutrition for us here.*

When Cray came later, I asked him for more of that fruit.

"No more," he said. "No more until next year. You like them?"

"Yes. There's something in them my body needs. Is there anything else like them?"

"I will see."

"If there isn't, I'll have to go back to my world where I can get proper nutrition. Peter and I are both losing strength in spite of exercising. We sleep longer than we used to. I eat tons of food and still don't feel full. And we're both losing weight."

"Not thin there." Cray pointed to my round belly.

I debated whether to tell him. I hadn't wanted to let anyone here know, but I trusted him and he was our only source of help. It would become obvious soon, anyway. Not knowing the word for 'pregnant', I *sent* him a picture of me with a tiny baby curled up in my stomach.

"Oh," he said, wide eyed. "We must take you to nursery where you belong."

"Not if they have the same food as I get here. Peter and I must return to our world, and soon."

"The Gatekeepers are not ready. You must wait."

His words filled me with terror. "I can't. I don't have time." I wrapped my arms around my belly. "Please."

Cray stared over my head. "I will ask," he said presently. "Now we do lesson."

Later, he did return with the name of the substance, but said it was not found in any other food as far as he could find out. Peter determined the makeup of the substance from Cray, and after Cray left, he began *searching* for it with his mind. He could only do a small area of the building at a time.

Five days later Peter *reached* a laboratory and *found* some of the substance. I'd lost a lot of my energy and could only sit and watch the screen. I begged Cray every time he came to let me go home. The baby barely moved, and she wasn't growing right.

It took Peter most of an afternoon to *move* the bottle from the lab to our room, waiting for people to open doors so he could *bring* it through. At floor level, nobody notice it.

When we ate, he tipped a tiny bit on my food and stirred it in.

Baby and I stopped going downhill, but it wasn't enough.

He kept the bottle with him, even sleeping with it, so I wouldn't try to take more. A couple days later I told Cray my baby was dying.

"I have to go home. Now."

"No," Cray said. "You must stay here until they tell us you are ready to leave."

"We'll be dead by then. We're already sick. What good will it do them for us to be too sick to do whatever it is they want?" I coughed and bent over.

"I will deal with that. Now read this."

Days passed. Peter doled out just enough to keep me going. I begged for more, but he said there wasn't that much.

Finally, after four days without him, Cray returned.

"We go now. Bring your things." With a burst of adrenalin, we followed him to the lift and down to the Gate. He did not respond to our questions. I prayed to the Oneness that we were going to Harmony and not another world.

Chapter 25   Back to Harmony

As the darkness faded, I realized that I was curled up on a round bed, in a much larger round room. The blue walls led up into a blue dome overhead. I fought to a sitting position. Sensing a wrongness, I checked myself and the baby. We were as well as we could be.

Peter stirred and sat up next to me.

"How do you feel, Petey?"

"Strange." He stretched. "Like someone took me apart and put me back together again, not quite the same."

"Likewise," Cray said, sitting up on a second bed. "This should be your world."

We climbed to our feet and followed Peter out of the single door into a long corridor. It was pale gray, well lit, and full of fresh, odorless air. The walls were blank, not even any doors, nothing to show how far we'd gone. Presently we came to a three way split and stopped.

"Okay, which way?" Peter asked.

We *reached* down each opening, but found nothing. Cray started down the right hand tunnel.

"Why this one?" I asked, following him, Peter behind me.

I *received* a picture of a maze in my mind, with a red line always going to the right. Cray led the way though several more junctions, always to the right, until we came to a long room with beds and tables. I dropped into the first seat I came to.

At the far end, two large windows showed open, hilly forest and bright sunshine. The space between, where a door should have been, was just plain tan wall. "How do we get out?" I asked.

Peter prowled around looking at things and touching the walls. Cray watched, then went to a nearby table and tapped a flat button in the wall just above it. A chime rippled, a small piece of wall slid aside, a tray on a folding arm slid out. The large platter of food on the tray slid off onto the table.

As the arm withdrew and the wall closed, we gathered around the food.

A large bowl on the platter piled high with steaming meats and vegetables was surrounded by fruits, and two large loaves of bread perched on top. Unfortunately, there was no wuva, the fruit I needed.

"Wow," Peter said. He picked up a loaf, tore it into three pieces, and took a big bite of one.

"Don't eat it all, we may need it later," I said, removing the fruits and putting them into my bag, along with the other loaf.

Cray found utensils and we dug into the hot stew. For the first time in a long time, I felt really full, and not nauseous for a change.

Peter tested the walls by the other tables, but nothing happened. I moved to the chair at the end by the window and stared out at a real live world.

Cray studied the wall between the windows and said, "This is not right. Should always have a way out."

Peter joined us. "You didn't find anything unusual about the windows?" I asked. Both men looked at me, then pawed around them randomly. Cray said something I didn't catch. They began feeling the frames in the same place at the same time, outside top corner to inside top corner and down.

Suddenly a vertical crack appeared and a door sized piece of wall slid aside. I grabbed my stuff and trotted out, followed by the men.

In a wide, grassy place surrounded by deep green hills, topped by a rich blue sky, I took a deep breath and *reached*. There was nothing except a few small creatures I didn't recognize, up in the forest. The air felt wrong. A ripple of terror slid over me.

"This is not Harmony," I said, turning to them.

"What, Perri?" Peter asked.

"The Gate was set to your world when we went into the Gate room," Cray said. We all looked back at the door and saw only hills. Peter and I ran over and scrabbled at the grass, but there was nothing under it but soil and rocks.

It was too much. I collapsed into a heap on the ground. How could we ever find our way off this world and to ours? Would my baby and I die on a strange world we knew nothing about? Peter squatted beside me and rubbed my shoulder.

"We'll get home, sis," he said.

Cray knelt down next to us.

"Maybe we can send message from here, all three of us," he said. We sat and held hands. Peter and I linked, brought Cray in, and *searched* for the Gate. Nothing. Then we *sent* as loud as we could, 'wrong world, wrong world, wrong world'.

"Should we stay here?' Peter asked after we caught our breath.

"No. Gate will not open with us out here. Can only go out, not in. We need to find another Gate," Cray said.

Peter ran up to the top of the nearest hill and looked around. "Nothing," he called.

"Which way downhill?" I asked.

"That way." Peter pointed toward the lowering sun. Cray helped me up and we headed down the sloping grass, which turned into scrub and rocks. I couldn't believe how hard it was to put one foot in front of the other, but I had no breath with which to speak. Even thinking was difficult.

As the sun dropped behind the hills, we found a little stream trickling along, and decided to camp there. My legs shook and all I could do was lie down and wrap myself in my cloak.

"At least we have water," Peter said. "And this place has a stronger gravity than the other ones we've been on."

"True," Cray agreed.

In the morning, we followed the stream downhill. I felt a bit stronger after my rest, but walking still felt like I had weights on my feet. I also felt lost and frustrated and scared. My baby was all right so far. But we'd come all this way and still weren't home, had no idea where we were, where there might be another Gate, when and where we might find more food. I kicked an inoffensive stone into the stream.

I took a deep breath and said, "We'll find a way, we have to, they wouldn't just leave us here to die."

"Why not?" Cray replied. "I am of no more use to them, and if they acquired what they wanted from you, they wouldn't care what happened to you."

"No," I said, stopping. "That can't be true." I refused to believe it. "We landed on their world without their knowing. If they have plans that don't involve us, why didn't they just come kill all of us? There'd be no point in leaving us here when there's hundreds more still on Harmony. We have to get back and warn our people."

"They could leave us here and go to Harmony and kill all the ones there," Peter said.

"Oh, stop it," I screamed, and burst into tears. Peter took me in his arms.

"Hush, sis, we'll make it." To Cray, "Why did they send us here when they could have just sent us home? It wouldn't have taken any more power."

"Power same, power source not."

"Oh." Peter nodded his head. "Well. Let's keep going." We started off along the stream, and soon reached deeper forest. "Hey," Peter said, stopping. "This looks like a trail." It was a narrow, well-trod path.

"Made by large animal," Cray said. I shivered. Now we had something else to watch out for. "Like in forest on Onan."

I *searched*, but couldn't *sense* any danger.

We continued on. Little chittering critters and humming things accompanied us, with occasional crashing in the underbrush in the distance. A piney smell mixed with something else tickled my nose. I struggled along and Peter gave me the biggest piece of bread at noon.

The sun was still up when we came to a glade where another stream joined ours. I collapsed from exhaustion. "Let's camp here," I muttered. "I can't go another inch." We ate more fruit and half of the remaining bread.

After a while I *reached* as far to the west as I could. At the very edge I found something more than just animal. Could it be a Gate? We knew there had to be another one on this world. I decided not to mention what I'd found until we got closer and I could tell what it was.

"What are we going to do for food?" Peter asked. I could tell he was still hungry.

"There are many things in the forest we can eat," Cray said.

"Will they give me and my child the nutrition we need?"

"I do not know."

#

Sometime in the night, I was half awakened by a noise, a movement, an uneasiness. I shifted, but could not completely wake or move. I sensed that I was being carried, and soon drifted off. A little later, the Oneness briefly connected me with Mama. I felt her waiting, half numb state. The next thing I knew, it was daylight and the men were stirring.

Chapter 26   On the Trail

I sat up and whispered, "Mama." I took a deep breath and blinked. The air tasted different. Slipping out of my blanket, I stole away into the trees. I didn't feel the pull that had kept dragging me down the past two days. After taking care of business, I found an open spot and *reached*. There was something, something familiar.

I couldn't believe it, I must be dreaming. But from something inside me, I knew. We were on Harmony. They'd moved us in the night, while we were sleeping. I trotted back to camp.

"Something wrong?" Peter mumbled, rubbing his eyes.

"No, something's right." I danced around him. "We're on Harmony." I wanted to fly away west.

"Huh?"

"We were moved in the night. It feels like Harmony and there's something out there." I pointed away from the rising sun.

Peter stumbled to his feet, looked around, trotted into the trees, and a few moments later ran out and around the camp. "It sure feels like Harmony."

"What is," Cray mumbled, rolling over onto his back.

"We're on Harmony."

He sniffed. "Yes, is different." He rose and took his turn in the woods.

We packed up and headed off at a trot until Cray stopped us. "Not so fast. We have several days," he said. We slowed down. My excitement overruled my hunger, for the time being. The stream led us westward.

Cray found a mark he'd made the first time he'd come. "The Gate was same as when I came through before," he said. "But door was not hidden. I hear sometimes Gate go to parallel universe. I think this is what happened to us."

"Then there are parallel universes." Peter said. "Uncle Art told me once some people on Earth thought there might be." I had no idea what they were talking about

"Yes."

"Wait 'til Uncle Art hears about this." Peter jumped for a tree limb and couldn't quite reach it.

In the afternoon, we came to a small grove of fruit trees, a kind I knew, but not the kind I needed. I'd have to get some of that soon. We ate two each and stuffed our pockets and bags.

The stream curled off to the south. We filled our water jugs and hiked up the ridge blocking it. All we could see beyond it were more ridges and a distant glitter. *Please, let it be the sea*, I thought.

We set up camp a little ways below the top.

I *reached* again. I found many sentient beings far to the west, but could not determine specific individuals. Sleep would not come until my baby reached out and calmed me.

In the morning, Peter and I *reached* together and touched the first Four. 'Mama?'

'Where you?'

'East.' We lost the connection. I wept into Peter's shoulder.

"So we're home." His voice shook. After a hug, "Come on, Perri, let's go." He trotted down into the valley, Cray behind him. I could not keep up, I was afraid I'd fall, and didn't have the energy. Finally Peter stopped to let us catch up.

"Cray, how far do you want to come with us," I asked after I caught my breath.

"I will stay with you until you meet your people."

It took us two days to descend, cross the valley and reach the top of the next ridge. Only then were we able to *reach* anyone. After we checked in with the Four, we collapsed into sleep.

The following day, down in the next valley, we found fish in the little river at the bottom, and Peter managed to entice them to the bank and grab them.

Cray had a firemaker, so we were able to cook the fish. They tasted so sweet I wished we had more. We followed the river north to where it came out of the hills, and had another fish for breakfast.

Climbing this ridge was harder, and I had to keep stopping to rest. Peter and Cray had to help me to the top, where I was too tired to even try to use my Talent. Again, I slept well.

I felt better in the morning, so Peter and I *reached*. Uncle Bay *answered*. Charley and Uncle Allen were with him, up past the trail to about where Peter had been taken. All I could do was soak in them.

'How are you?' Uncle Bay *sent.*

'Not much food, Perri sick,' Peter *answered.*

'I'm okay,' I *added.*

'Where are you?'

'Another valley, more hills, lower in south,' Peter *said.*

'Can you keep going?'

'Oh yes,' I *said.*

I *sensed* through Uncle Bay that Mama was literally jumping for joy and trying to persuade Papa to come meet us.

'Hang in there. We've got extra supplies,' Charley *sent.* 'You know Uncle Allen never gets lost. See you soon, love.'

I sank back in Peter's arms, and we both sat down.

"Charley's coming for us," I said, not quite believing it.

#

We continued on. Another ridge top, another sunny day, another meal of grass. We sat and watched the forest on the hills across the way, the sun warming our backs. Somewhere out there, Charley was coming to get me. I wanted to run down and meet him, but my body refused to move.

Even Peter wasn't moving, and he was stronger than me and not carrying a baby. I fretted about her, was the lack of food hurting her, or was she pulling nutrition out of my body? All I could do now was wait. At least we were on our way home.

Peter woke me from a doze. "Look, there they are." He pointed to a bare spot near the top of the other ridge. Three people moved along it. I could only tell who they were, not contact them. Peter jumped up and waved.

'Soon,' I *heard* faintly.

Cray rose. "I leave you now. I will follow behind. You need not tell others of me."

"Where will you go?" I asked, turning to look up at him.

"Near you, in forest. I remember a place from last time. Listen for me." He turned and walked back down the way we'd come. He would still be with us.

After the sun passed overhead, we saw our rescuers down in the valley. Peter picked up my cloak and said, "Let's go meet them. It's downhill."

He helped me to my feet and we started down.

Chapter 27   A Fall and Charley

After getting the juices flowing, I pulled away. I could still walk by myself, even though I was feeling queasy. I figured it was the baby; I was aware of her all the time now.

There was no real path, and Cray wasn't here to guide us. We just picked our way down between the rocks and scattered bushes. Every once in a while I looked down to see where Charley and the others were.

When one of the men below pulled out in front I forgot to look where I was putting my foot, and tripped on a good sized rock at the top of a drop. I went sailing, but managed to slow myself a bit to land on my left knee and fall over onto my side.

My child was fine, but I wasn't. Peter just missed catching me, and I *felt* his anguish.

He scrambled down beside me. "Are you all right? Your knee is bleeding." He fumbled in the cloak pockets.

I hauled myself up to a sitting position, clasped my hands over the abrasion, and focused on blood clotting. Peter came up with a bit of bandage.

"You fell slow, almost like you were flying." Peter patted my shoulder. I eased away from my focus and controlled my breathing. "We'll wait here for them," he added. I leaned into him with my good shoulder, trying not to think, *feeling* Charley's presence mingling with Peter's, as he led the three rushing up the hill to us.

Presently I heard voices calling, via Peter, thudding footsteps, and Charley's panting as he dropped down in front of me. "Charley," I whispered, and reached for him, shaking, tears streaming down my face. The other two knelt beside him.

"Perri," Charley choked, "my love. Don't ever do this again."

'I'm home' washed over me.

Charley held me out. "You're so thin. Where have you been?"

"Later," I mumbled. All I wanted was to feel him with me now. He saw my knee and shrugged off his pack as Uncle Bay and Uncle Allen had done with theirs. He pulled open the tear in my pant leg, gently rubbed salve on the wound, and wrapped a long strip of bandage cloth around it.

'So that's why you wouldn't let me touch it,' Peter *sent*. I ignored him. He'd been talking to Uncle Bay, but I didn't hear what they said.

"What happened?" Uncle Bay asked.

"I tripped and fell, but I'll be okay."

Peter's stomach growled. "You guys got any food? We haven't eaten anything for days."

"Sure, here." Uncle Allen pulled out a couple pouches of bread soaked in broth. Peter gobbled his down, but I only ate half of mine. I closed my eyes, concentrated, and kept it down.

"Thanks, Uncle Allen," I said. "Good to see you guys." Uncle Bay brought me into the Four, and I touched Mama briefly, letting her know we were back. She hadn't eaten for days either. They welcomed us and let us go.

Charley scooted around so he could hold me in his arms, and we all just sat and breathed the lovely mountain air. After a while, feeling better, I made a move to get up. Charley held me down. "Rest," he said, and gave me a gentle squeeze.

"It's hot, just sitting here in the sun," I said.

"Son, let's make a tent," Uncle Bay said. Together, and with the Four, he and Charley produced a clear bubble of energy that covered all of us. Instantly it was cooler and not as bright.

"You never told me about this, Charley," I said, looking up at his face. He grinned. "How long are we going to stay here?" Now that I'd connected with Mama, I wanted to get home as soon as possible.

"Have you checked your injuries?" Uncle Bay asked.

"Not really." I closed my eyes and looked inward. "There's something torn in my knee, and my shoulder hurts, but nothing's broken. The pain's not bad." I had learned a long time ago how to control pain, in myself and others.

Uncle Bay looked around, picked me up and carried me to a grassy hollow just below where we sat. The bubble and the men followed. After getting me settled, he and Charley splinted my knee.

"We'll camp here and head back in the morning," Uncle Bay said. "We could use the rest, too. Don't worry, we have plenty of food. Gabe and Han will start out as soon as they can get ready, and meet us on the way back. Allen, you've had some medical training, see what you think."

Uncle Allen poked around my shoulder and moved my arm a little. I bit back a yelp. "I think it's just bruised," he said. "Try not to move your arm too much. This'll help." He took another long bandage and tied my arm to my body and made a sling for my forearm.

As the sun eased down behind the hills, we talked and ate. I wasn't ready to discuss my adventures, so Peter and I asked about what had been going on back home. I leaned against Charley, drawing warmth and strength from him. Peter reclined on my other side, with me on our special link. And I *sensed* Mama holding onto me while Papa fed her.

"No major disasters," Uncle Allen said. "The crops are down because of the low river and less than normal rain. A number of young couples, both Terran and Bramite, have gone up to the north settlement and begun building homes up there, without the approval of the council. Unfortunately, they weren't prepared, and we lost one of the young Bramite women in childbirth."

"I started building us a house up there," Charley said, "but I had to quit and come home when I began having nightmares about horrible things happening to you."

"Oh, Charley," I said, touched.

I learned from Uncle Bay that the word had gotten around about our absence, and some of the more conservative Bramites pulled further back into their private places. A group of them had headed south and not yet returned. Mama had tried to reach Judee, but she was too ill, and Dela refused to talk to Mama.

Adam had drawn into himself, did his duties, but never laughed. Kareth and her children, except for Gabe, left him alone. She told Mama one day that when she tried to get him to love her, Adam pushed Kareth away and ran out of the house. Mama didn't say, but I had a feeling that he might have approached Mama about having another child.

Later, I said, "You guys must have really been pushing it."

"We did," Charley said. "Couldn't wait to see you."

"I like this," Uncle Bay added. "Quiet, away from people."

"I thought you could shut it out," I said.

"Not completely. Here, with just us, I can, but not back in the community. I can mute it down to a low level, but it's still always there. You are indeed ahead of us. Can you shut down, Peter?"

"Yeah, down to where it's just background noise I can ignore."

"In the city, I had to totally shut down, except for a tiny tendril to find Peter. Otherwise I couldn't think at all," I said.

"What city?" Charley asked. "Where were you guys?"

"Perri, Peter, would you be willing to share your experiences with the rest of the Fours?" Uncle Bay asked.

"Well, I thought we'd wait until we got home. It's such a muddle."

"Why not do it now. We're linked, and the others aren't busy with duties, if you don't mind sharing with Allen."

"Only if he swears to never say one word about it to anyone except us. This has to stay among us Fours. Don't want to create a panic," I said.

"I swear," Uncle Allen said, smiling. Although from Mama's side of the family, Uncle Allen looked like Uncle Bay's younger brother.

Peter and I *opened up* and *let them in*, only concealing the fact that Cray had come with us to Harmony. Afterward, as the stars blinked on, we sat in silence for a while. Peter and I ate a bit more, and curled into sleep.

Chapter 28   Rain and Reunion

In the morning, Peter and I were ready to go, even though I felt stiff all over. My knee wouldn't hold me, so Charley half carried me, swinging me along on my good leg. We stopped to rest often, and Charley and Uncle Bay insisted that Peter and I eat something every time we stopped.

"It's so great to be here with you," I said, finally enjoying the outdoors.

When we reached the forest on the other side of the stream in the valley, I asked, "Can one of you make me a crutch out of one of these branches?"

"Sure," Uncle Allen said. We stopped for an afternoon snack, and he picked out branches and carved them into crutches, having me stand with them to get the height right. He made the left one so it fitted under my armpit and around front, so my arm leaned on it. There was a little knob on the end for my hand to hold on to and lift the crutch.

They were fine on the flat area where we were, but going uphill was much slower, as I had to pull myself up each step. Charley walked on my left side and kept a hand on the back of my waist in case I slipped. Peter and Uncle Allen trotted up the trail, and had to keep stopping to wait for us to catch up.

Uncle Bay said he was glad to go slowly; he hadn't done a lot of hiking in the last few years.

I kept up an on and off conversation with Mama, through the Fours. Our Four had clicked back together as soon as Charley, Peter, and I had *reached* Gabe.

Mama couldn't sit still, darting from one thing to another, even dancing like a young girl. She *told* me that Papa said he hadn't seen her so wound up since they found the tunnel exit from Nubram, where they'd lived with the Bramites.

"That was so far away and so long ago," Mama said.

"Yeah, and here we are, waiting for your kids to come home," Papa said.

"Our kids and don't you forget it."

Way to go, Mama, I thought, and shut down. I didn't like to intrude. It was cool in the forest, and I crutched on, content, with Charley at my side.

We stopped early for the night, and I asked, "How are we doing for food?"

"We still have plenty," Uncle Bay said. "Rest now."

#

Uncle Allen had marked the way well. The next two days we worked our way northward and up along a ridge. Although I felt little pain, I was frustrated about how slow we were going. I kept trying to speed up, only to be pulled back by Charley.

We passed one of the guys' campsites, and on the third night we stayed at one where they'd left some extra bags of food and stuff.

From the top of the ridge I stared at the distant sea, but it seemed as far away as ever. My little one continued to grow and thrive, and I felt stronger. Eating our own food was giving us the nutrition we needed.

"How much longer?" I asked as we ate. Even though the scrape on my knee was healing nicely, I still couldn't put any weight on that leg. The shoulder only hurt if I jarred or hit it, but I knew it was healing. I still wanted to see Noa, which I'd told Mama. I was still sometimes queasy in the mornings, but so far kept everything down.

"Another couple days or so," Charley said, brushing my hair back and kissing my cheek.

In the morning, we woke to cold and gray skies, and a little before noon we felt raindrops. Uncle Bay suggested we stop, but the rest of us want to continue on.

"It's only a few drops," I said, putting on my cloak. As we kept going, the rain picked up. Suddenly I slipped on the wet ground and twisted my bad knee. Charley caught me, but not in time. The splint refused to stay in place.

My yelp startled everyone. Peter raced back from where he'd gone ahead, slipped, and slid down on his bottom. I laughed, and the pain went away.

"Be careful," Uncle Allen said, yanking Peter to his feet. "We don't need any more injured people to carry home."

"Over here," Uncle Bay said. He and Charley set up the bubble over a soft area and covered all of us. We sat on his dry ground cloth. As Charley held me, I massaged my knee and subdued the pain.

"Maybe I should carry her," Charley said.

"How long could you do that?" his dad asked. "What would happen if you slipped?"

"I won't slip."

"No, we'll stay here until the rain stops."

"What if it's one of those storms that goes on for days?" Peter asked. Uncle Bay glared at him, and we settled down.

Rain fell the rest of the day and into the night. When I *talked* to Mama, she said the storm had come through there the day before. All of us, except Peter, woke and moved around several times during the night. I wondered how Cray was doing in the rain. Probably curled up under a nice, tight bush.

The next morning the rain had stopped, and I saw a bit of blue sky in the west. "Let's go," I said. "My knee's better." We ate quickly, packed up and moved on. Uncle Allen led the way, as usual, to make sure we stayed on the trail. It was fairly level here, and we soon came to a river.

"This is our river," Uncle Bay said. "All we have to do now is follow it down."

I was ready to run, if I could have.

"Too bad we don't have a boat," Peter said. "We could float down the river."

"Not from here," Uncle Allen said. "There's a waterfall and a couple of narrows full of rocks."

Uncle Bay dropped back behind us, and far behind him I *sensed* Cray. I wanted to dance for joy, but that was out of the question, too. So I sang, until Peter told me to shut up. Then I sang to him on our link until he unlinked.

Late that afternoon, we found the men's first night camp, well above the trail. Gabe and Han were waiting for us. I wanted to keep going, even though I could hardly move, but Uncle Bay insisted on camping there.

Gabe joined with Charley, Peter and me to remake our Four in person. Afterward, Gabe said, "We seem to be five, now."

"Yes," I said, and a part of me wished she was his. He smiled at me and strode into the woods. Charley moved uneasily, but said nothing.

I *contacted* Mama to let her know where we were.

'We'll come up in the morning to meet you.'

'Can you get Noa to come? My knee's still pretty bad.'

'I'll see what I can do. Sleep tight. I love you.' I felt her joy bubbling out.

As tired as I was, I could not sleep. So many things went through my mind. The places I'd been, the people and nonpeople I'd met, all the things I'd seen. I'd had no idea there was so much out there. Mama's worlds hadn't been real, like these. I wondered what kind of worlds would my daughter find?

Daughter. Girl child. It was still hard for me to grasp that I was going to become a mother, do all those mama things. Although I'd been around many babies, I had no idea what I needed to do, or how to do them.

I'd found a new friend, Cray, different from my others, but a real person. And I still couldn't figure out why they'd taken Peter in the first place. If it was to see what we're like, why did they just dump him in a room and leave him?

Had they wanted to lure me in, they could have just come and gotten me too. But then, later, there was all that poking and prying. And although Cray was much like us, his mindlink was different, but we could still communicate. And the way they raised their kids--I like ours better.

After *receiving* our experiences, Aunt Pauli had *said* that at least that way all the children were cared for properly. Too many parents on her Earth apparently didn't know how to raise their children.

In between one thought and another, I slipped into sleep.

Chapter 29   Home at Last

I woke before the sun was up and rushed everyone through breakfast and breaking camp. In the back of my mind, I *sensed* Mama, Noa, and Amy starting for the trail. Amy, Uncle Adam's eldest daughter, had as much energy as the other two. Noa had delivered three difficult babies the day before.

Charley had to hold me back. I kept stumbling in my haste to get home. The warm, bright day fed me energy, and only my knee kept me from pulling away and running. And Mama was coming. I would see her today.

I didn't want to stop for lunch, but both Uncle Bay and Charley insisted.

"I'll go on ahead," Peter suggested.

"No." Uncle Bay said. "We'll stay together."

We continued to follow the river until we reached the top of the trail where Mama, Noa, and Amy met us.

"Mama," I yelled. She ran up to me and gathered me into her arms. Peter hugged both of us.

"My babies," Mama crooned, tears of joy running down her face. "But you're so thin."

"We didn't have much to eat until we met up with Uncle Bay and them," Peter said. "Where's Papa?"

"Come," Noa said, gently pulling me away and sitting me down on a handy log. "Let me look at your knee." She carefully touched and felt around it. "Definitely something torn in there. When you get home, you'll have to stay off it awhile."

"How long?"

"Depends on how it heals. Do what you can to help it."

"Hi, kids," Papa said, coming out of the forest.

Mama spun around. "What are you doing here?" she demanded.

"I told you I wasn't going to let you come up here by yourself."

He gave us a big hug. "We'd better get moving if we want to get home before dark." He grabbed Mama's hand.

Charley and Noa helped me to my feet. Amy took my cloak. Uncle Allen and Peter went on ahead. Mama and Papa let the others go next, including Charley and me, and came along behind us. Bay brought up the rear. I blushed when I *sensed* Mama thinking that we did make a lovely couple.

About halfway down, we met Aunt Pauli and the rest of her children. She hugged Charley and me at the same time, and turned to Uncle Bay. Beth hugged me and stayed by my side, pouring out questions. She was bigger than I was, and starting to waddle. The rest of the kids gravitated to Uncle Allen.

We continued on down, meeting most of the rest of the Terrans on the way. I felt Uncle Bay slipping off into the forest as I shut down my mind and let my body slump. I wasn't prepared for the crowd that welcomed us home. Charley and Papa carried me through the groups of people, followed by Mama and Peter, up to the cabin.

Noa said she'd come see me the next day and slipped off to her clinic. Uncle Adam met us on the way to the cabin. He hugged me, then Peter, and told Mama to take care of us. He excused us from our duties until we were well. After a last, searching look, he strode away.

"May I stay?" Charley asked. "I can sleep on the floor. I'm used to it, and Perri needs me."

"Certainly," Mama said. "She needs all the loving she can get." She dropped onto the couch. Charley and Papa carried me into my old room and sat me down on my bed.

"I need a bath," I said.

"We all do," Charley said, kissing me.

As Peter set up the big tub, Mama fetched pots of hot water and some cleaning cloths. She shooed Charley out, helped me get my clothes off, and washed as much of me as she could. We decided that my hair could wait for another day. She touched my round belly. "How is she?"

"She's fine, Mama. I think she has some kind of protection besides my body. I fell, and I was able to consciously slow it and roll so I landed on my side and not my front." I looked at Mama's face. Was that a wrinkle by her eye? "Mama, what am I turning into?"

"You're becoming an intelligent young woman with a unique Talent. Have you picked a name for her yet?"

'Marisa,' came into our minds from outside. Or was it inside?
"All right, Marisa it is," I said.

After a pause, while Mama worked on my legs, I said, "What is my child going to be like? Will she have more Talent than I do?"

Mama paused and looked at me. "Yes, I'd say so. The people in my generation are beyond our parents, your generation is beyond mine, so she should be beyond yours. And the first born seems to be the strongest. Have you had any morning sickness?"

I rolled my eyes. "Too much. Oh, Mama, I'm so scared."

"That's normal, especially for the first time. Fortunately, Peter popped out right on your heels."

"I don't mean that. I mean after, raising her. What do I do when her Talent gets to where I can't handle her?"

"Do what I did. Raise her as a normal child, keep track of everything she does that may indicate a Talent. Let me know, and we'll work together with her. But probably she won't show much until she gets near puberty, like you and Peter."

"I remember." I leaned back on my pillow. "Thanks, Mama."

"Now you go to sleep. Charley will be here, literally at your feet, if you need anything in the night." She kissed my cheek, brushed my forehead. "I love you."

"Me too," I murmured. Charley, wearing old clothes of Papa's, much too short, brought in his sleeping blankets, dropped them on the floor, and leaned over and kissed me. I reached up with my good arm to hug him.

"I love you so much," he whispered, and curled up in his blankets. I *sensed* Mama tucking Peter in, and settled into my pillows. I was home at last, but somehow I knew this was just the beginning.

PART THREE - ALIENS

Chapter 30   First Day Back

I woke up wondering why the ground was so soft, and remembered. I was home. I sat up and yelped as my sore shoulder jerked. I couldn't move my leg. "Mama," I called.

"I'm here," Charley said, watching me from a nearby chair. He came over, kissed me, and asked, "How are you this morning, love?"

"I ache all over and I have to pee." Charley picked me up to carry me to the outhouse. We ran into Mama in the doorway.

She stepped back and said, "First things first."

Afterward, Charley set me on the couch and propped up my leg. Mama sat beside me.

"How are you, dear?" she said, as if she couldn't tell.

"I feel like I've been through a mill wheel," I said. I *felt* her wince. "But I'm really happy to be home. I'm not going to be able to do much for a while, but I'll do what I can."

"You'd better stay here for a few days, so I can look after you. Charley, you can stay here too, if you want."

He muttered something. I looked around for the others. Peter was probably still sleeping, and I guessed Papa had already gone to work.

"You two must be hungry." Mama bustled off to the kitchen.

"I want you home with me," Charley said.

"Are you going to be there if I need something?"

"Well, I'll have to go back to work tomorrow."

"Then I better stay here with Mama, in case I need something, like a chamber pot." I didn't want to sit in my house alone all day. No one except Mama had much time to sit with an invalid. And her house was more central.

Charley grumbled, and carried me over to the table. The eggs and toast tasted wonderful, and I kept it down. He watched every bite I took, in between his forkfuls.

After we were done, Mama told us Doc and Noa were coming over in a little while. Charley settled me on the couch and took off to get us some clean clothes. Mama washed up the dishes, then sat with me until Doc and Noa arrived.

"Let's see that knee," Doc said, unwrapping it. The area around it was a lovely shade of purple. He poked and prodded and moved the knee. "I'm not a knee man, but something feels loose in there. Best keep off of it for a while. How does it feel inside?"

"Something's disconnected, but the bones feel okay."

"How's the shoulder doing?"

"Still sore. Hurts when I move or touch it."

"It'll take a while for that to heal, too." He moved away and sat down. "Your turn, Noa."

Noa rubbed salve into my knee and leg, then into other parts of my scratched up body. Next, she used the stethoscope to listen to the baby. "Nice, strong heartbeat," she said. "You need to lead a nice, quiet life the next few months."

"Ha," I said.

"Lyn, try to keep her off her feet as much as possible."

"I'll do what I can."

Charley returned, wearing fresh clothes, carrying others in a bag. "How is she, doc?"

"She'll live. Cold water on that knee might help get the swelling down. Too bad we don't have ice packs here. Wet cloths will have to do." He creaked to his feet and took his leave. Charley stared after him.

"I have to stay off my foot and it'll take a while to heal," I said. "By the time I can get around, I'll be too big to move much."

Mama fetched a big pot and put it under my raised knee, then brought cold wet cloths to drape over it, letting them drip into the pot below.

A little later Uncle Art popped in. "How ya doing?" he said, squatting in front me. He pulled out a tape and measured my knee and leg. He had the square Harlan face, and his tied back hair hung long and straight down his back. "I think I know what I can make a brace out of," he said, noting down figures.

Peter wandered out yawning. "What's up?"

"My knee, sleepyhead," I said.

"Good morning," Mama said. "Are you hungry?"

"Am I ever." His stomach growled. Mama brought him food as Uncle Art left.

Charley sat down beside me and asked Mama, "Aunt Lyn, you sure I can't take her home?"

"I'm quite sure. I know what you've got in mind, and she's not ready for that yet." Ha, I thought. "Give her a couple more days."

He put his arm around me, and I felt his warmth and desire. I wanted him, too, but knew that Mama wasn't going to leave us alone. I pushed him away and made sure by mindlink that he understood.

"Have you heard from Judee lately?" I asked Mama.

"No, and Dela won't talk to me. Do you feel up to trying to reach her?"

"I think so. Maybe with your help."

Charley kissed me, rose, and left. Mama took his place and we *focused*.

'Dela, it's me, Perri. Do you hear me?'

'Hey, where you been?'

I gave her a brief description of my adventures, and added, 'I can't go anywhere for a while, so I hope everything's okay up there. How's your Mama?'

'She hardly leaves her tree anymore. I don't know what I'm going to do when she's gone.'

'You'll manage. Call if you need anything.'

Mama and I looked at each other. She *shared* her sadness at Judee's condition, and the memory of when they first met, in the huge hotel on Centralia. Mama had gotten lost in the maze of corridors, and somehow ended up at Judee's room. The two had become firm friends.

I dozed 'til dinner, then Aunt Pauli came by afterward. "How are you doing? And where's that son of mine?"

"Better. Things still hurt, and I'm too tired to do anything, but I'm so happy to be home with everyone. Except I'm getting bored and I hate mending."

Aunt Pauli laughed, and put the basket she was carrying beside me on the couch. "Here's some little pastimes I've been making for the children. Maybe they'll amuse you a bit."

"Thanks, Aunt Pauli."

She went off to talk to Mama, and I took a little puzzle thing from the basket.

I was still playing with it when Uncle Art returned with the brace. It took a little while to get it to fit properly. Mama had to find some stuff for padding around the knee. It went halfway up my thigh and halfway down my shin. He helped me stand on my good foot and moved my leg back and forth from the hip.

"Looks good. Where are your crutches?" Mama fetched them out of my room, and I took a couple tentative steps, my bad leg swinging. "Looks good," Uncle Art repeated. "How does it feel?"

"Okay, I guess." My forearm leaned on the left crutch, but I still felt little pulls in my bad shoulder. I turned around, crutched back to the couch and sat down. "I'll have to work on this."

"Try to go at least a couple steps more each time," Mama said. "Thank you, Art."

"No sweat. Take it easy." He left.

The rest of the day passed slowly. Charley came and went, but ate supper with us. Mama wouldn't let him in my room until she thought I was asleep.

Chapter 31   At Mama's

Over the next two days, I practiced walking with the brace and the crutches, and on the second afternoon, I made it to the outhouse by myself. Mama got me some baskets to weave, and lots of people came by to bring get well wishes, food, and things to keep me occupied. It was an event in our circle, someone hurt and unable to do her duties.

On the third morning, Charley and I told Mama that we were going home to our house that night.

"Wait til Doc checks you," Mama said. "He's coming this morning."

"Okay." I was planning to wait 'til after supper anyway, so I wouldn't have to cook, but I knew Charley wanted to go right away. He went off to his duties. I read one of Mama's old Earth books, *The Wizard of Oz*.

Doc came just before lunch and said everything was healing nicely, and he saw no reason why I couldn't go to my house that night.

Charley protested about staying for supper, and I asked him what we had at the house.

"I don't know." He shrugged. "Okay, we'll eat here, but we're leaving right after." He ate without stopping to talk, but I chatted with Mama and Papa, and he had to wait for me. Charley held me up on my foot as I hugged my folks, thanked them for their help, and took me away. I insisted on crutching the whole way, not that far, and felt his frustration.

I was surprised to see how clean and tidy our house was, until Charley told me how both of our mamas were over most every day. We headed for the bed. After finding a position that wouldn't hurt me, we let go.

Later, I nestled against him, soaking up his essence. Now that I was home, I realized that I had fallen in love with him while I was gone.

Chapter 32   The 'Cold'

The next morning, I sat up and sneezed. Charley looked at me, mouth open. "What was that?" I said, and my voice felt funny.

"You sneezed," Charley said, sitting up beside me. "Say something else."

"Why? Okay, now that I can get around, when can I go back to my duties?" I sneezed again, and my nose felt stuffy.

"You sound funny. How do you feel?"

"Tireder than yesterday. My head's stuffy. And I'm not hungry." I checked the baby. "She's okay, but something's attacking my insides."

"You stay here and rest. I'll get Doc or Noa to come see you." He crawled out of bed and prepared for the day. I used the outhouse and went back to bed.

After Charley left, I *reached* for Peter. He was sneezing, too. 'Tell Mama I've got what you've got.' For some reason I didn't feel like talking to Mama. Probably because she'd insist I come back to her house.

Doc came by midmorning and said it looked like a bad cold. "All I can tell you to do for it is rest, drink lots of water, and anything you can do to help your body heal itself. I told Peter and Lyn to stay home, and when Charley comes back, tell him I said he was to stay here."

"Why?"

"If it's anything like a cold, it'll spread fast. There are viruses in the drops you sneeze out, and if someone else breathes them in, they'll get infected and sick. You'll have several days of sniffling and sneezing and feeling under the weather before it goes away." He stopped and took a breath. "How long has it been since you left that other place?"

"Um." I quickly *asked* Peter. "Peter says seven days."

"Okay. If we get through the next several days and no one else gets sick, we may get through this without much trouble."

He fetched me a mug of water and made me drink it. "I'll be back this evening." He looked at me with a bemused smile. "I never thought I'd be making house calls in my old age."

"You're not old."

"Little one, I was old when we came here. But I'm planning to stick around for a while. See you later."

I was dozing when Mama came in. "How are you? How's your stomach?" she demanded.

Blinking, I sat up. "Oh, hi, Mama. I'm not hungry. Marisa's okay. I set up a blocker in the stuff that goes to her."

"Good," Mama breathed. I'd *felt* her sudden terror. "No one's been sick since the last cold went around when we first got here. We have to keep it from being serious. Can you control it at all, Perri?" She moved a cup on the table.

"Only to keep it from the baby. It came on when I was asleep."

Mama nodded. "Do you feel like walking down home? I don't like the idea of you being sick up here all alone."

I was a little scared myself, so I agreed to go. Would I ever feel like my old self again? Even though we went slowly, I was exhausted by the time we got home. I dropped beside Peter on the couch and slumped against him. He sneezed.

"I hate this," he said.

"At least you can walk, and your shoulder doesn't hurt so you can lay down any way you want."

"Big deal." He leaned his head back and closed his eyes. I dozed, too.

Charley and Doc arrived just before supper.

"Running back to Mama again," Charley said, as Doc spoke to Mama.

"I can't run and you know it." I folded my arms.

Doc turned. "Now, Charley. This is something new and we can't take chances leaving anyone sick off by themselves. You'll get her back in a few days."

Charley grunted and sat where he could watch me. Doc began checking Peter and me, listening to our hearts and lungs. "I don't hear any congestion," he said. "Still looks like a bad cold. Any coughing?"

"No," we said.

"My throat's a little scratchy," I added.

"I smell something tasty there, Lyn," Doc said. "I want you all to eat as much as you can. Fuel to feed your drives."

Papa stomped in, and Doc told him about the bug. "Oh, Christ, that's all we need. With Allen and Bay and Charley gone for several days, things have got screwed up. We can't afford to have people get sick now. You two brought it back with you, I gather?"

"Sorry, Papa," Peter said.

"Now, when you were in that other place," Doc began, "were you around anyone who was sniffling and sneezing?"

"No," I said. Peter shook his head.

"Hm. Were you ever poked and prodded like I do when I check you out?"

"Yes," I said, sitting up straight. "Just before the last gate. We were asleep, and when we woke we felt like we'd been stuck with all sorts of stuff. Who knows what they did to us."

"Sore all over," Peter mumbled.

"That's what Cray meant." I rocked back and forth. "They want to get rid of all of us because we're polluting this world of theirs. Cray's first visit was just to check it out, see how it was doing."

"No," Doc said.

"Yes. Why else would they have kept us there instead of killing us or sending us right back?"

"No," Mama said. I felt her understanding what I'd meant. "This is our home and no one's going to take it away from us or destroy us." Her green eyes glittered. "I won't let them."

"We won't let them," I said. "That's why they kept you in that cell, Petey, to lure me in. I was the one who Cray saw."

"I don't suppose you heard anything about a disease like this?" Doc asked.

"No."

"How dare they use my children like this," Mama burst out. "Is there anything you can give them?"

"No. Not knowing what kind of bug it is, most likely a virus, there's nothing I can do except repeat what I said this morning. Rest and drink lots of water. Let your bodies heal themselves. You two are young and healthy."

"Not everyone is," Mama said. She and I both thought of Alice, Doc's wife, old and feeble, mostly bedridden. She was the oldest person in the community.

Doc winced, shook his head, and creaked to his feet. "Watch yourselves, you and Larry. I need to get back to Alice. Holler if you need me. I'll come by tomorrow." He shuffled out and down the path.

"Come, let's eat," Mama said, rising. She served the stew. Peter and I ate about half of what we normally ate, but it did taste good. Afterward, Charley announced that he was taking me home.

"If she's not better in the morning, I'll bring her down here," he said as we left.

#

I spent the next two days at Mama's, and by the end of the second day, was feeling more like my normal self. Peter was still sick, and we had to practically pour water into his mouth to get him to drink.

The evening of the second day, I told Mama I was moving back to my house, but I'd *call* her if I needed anything. Charley was quiet when he took me home, and we did a lot more snuggling than usual before we made love. I wondered if he was coming down sick.

In the morning, he could hardly get out of bed. I *called* Mama and told her to let everyone know it was contagious. I would stay here and take care of him, but if Doc could come by sometime today, I'd appreciate it.

Doc showed up in the afternoon, and said that both Bay and Allen had come down with it too. "I've taken Noa away from her clinic, and your folks will be next, Perri," he said. "I told Adam, and he told the people up north to stay there."

The next day Mama started to sniffle. Papa came over and got us, helping Charley, who could hardly walk. It scared me to see him so sick. I fixed him up on the couch and went into to see Mama. Propped up on the big bed, she had a damp cloth on her face.

"I was going to wash all the used cloths today," she said. "Are you up to doing it? Peter's going through them like food, and this is the last one."

"Sure, Mama. I'm lots better today. You take care of yourself. I'll be here." I kissed her forehead and left.

Papa helped me set up the wash tub and fetched water.

"Where's Peter?" he asked.

"I haven't seen him." I closed my eyes. "Oh, he's up on the ridge." 'Petey, get your sorry ass home right now. Papa wants you,' I *told* him.

"Do you think this bug will kill anyone?" I asked Papa.

"No. You two are almost over it already. This bug is what we called a cold back on Earth, all sniffly and sneezy. Just about everyone got one at least once a year."

I looked at him. "You mean I could get it again? Doc was telling us that once you get a disease, you're immune, because your body's been insulated against it." I dropped the bundle of cloths.

He picked them up. "Some, yeah. But with our colds, there were so many different viruses, you could get a new one every time. Here, it's just the one, so you shouldn't get it again."

"That sounds better," I said.

Papa poured the water into the tub, I dumped the cloths in and picked up the soap.

"Probably everyone will get it, be sick for a few days, then it'll be gone," Papa said. I felt him watching me. "But we don't really know," he added.

"Why would they give us something that only makes us a little sick?" I wondered as I scrubbed.

"Testing, maybe, to see how much will wipe us out. If they thought what they gave you was a fatal dose, they seriously underestimated us."

"I don't know. There's something more to this, I think."

"To what?" Peter asked, charging up to us. "What do you need, Papa?"

"I need you to stay here for the time being. Where have you been?"

"Around. Had to get out of here for a while."

"You were supposed to stay home. Your mother is sick."

"I didn't know. I feel okay," Peter scuffed his toe in the pine needles.

Papa took him by the arm and led him away. "Peter, this is a new thing here. We don't know what's going to happen next. As long as you live under our roof, we expect you to follow our rules."

Peter mumbled something and went into the house. I grinned at the wash water as Papa returned.

"How are you feeling, Papa?"

"I'm fine. Can you handle this all right?"

"Sure." I'd propped myself up against the tub on the bench, my lower leg on a box.

He turned toward the house and sneezed. I shook my head and kept on scrubbing.

#

When Doc came by that evening, he was sniffling. "Same as you kids," he said. "Pauli's with Alice. Noa's down with it, so if any of you need a doctor in the next few days, you'll have to find one of the youngsters."

As Papa had forecast, the bug made its rounds. People were shuffled around to cover for the sick, and some things didn't get done. Fortunately, the children didn't get it as badly as the adults.

The people up in North Point ran short on supplies, so a group took some up to the halfway camp. Uncle Allen said the rock looked just like it always did. His people watched as the North Point group waved, picked up the bags of foodstuffs and left. No one up there got the bug—the first time.

Only two people died, a newborn preemie and his mother in childbirth. Noa told us she didn't think the baby would have survived anyway.

Those who were well tended the crops and ran the mill. School was closed for the duration. Most women were taking care of their families and had little time to do much for the community.

I stayed at my house or Mama's. Even going that short distance was a strain. My shoulder healed, and Noa had me doing exercises with it, what Doc called range of motion. I still couldn't put any weight on my knee. I wanted to throw the crutches away and run, but didn't dare.

Marisa grew fast, making it even harder for me to walk very far. Mama asked if I was sure I wasn't carrying twins.

"No, Mama, there's just one." At least I was past morning sickness and could eat as much as I wanted.

I *checked* with Cray. He'd gotten the bug, recovered, and was keeping an eye out for strangers.

It seemed the bug had left us, as people got well and the community eased back into normal routine.

Chapter 33   Last Meeting with Judee

After Mama got well, I *called* Dela. She said her mother wanted us to come up and see her. 'I can't walk very far, my leg's still bad," I said. "Can she, or you, fly your shuttle down here?'

We agreed to meet at a meadow near the mouth of the river. Charley came with us, he wouldn't leave my side. We saw the shuttle as we approached, near a stand of trees. Dela came to meet us, but stepped back when she saw Charley. "Who he?"

"My mate, Charley. Since the alien came, new rules are that all women leaving the settlement must have male escorts."

"Oh. Come." She led us to Judee, lying in a wide sling hung between two trees. She wore all her finery, for Mama.

"Oh, Judee," Mama said, taking her hand. Dela moved away and I followed.

"Charley, this is going to be boring girl talk, so go have a seat somewhere," I told him. He wandered over to look at the shuttle.

While I told Dela about my adventures, I also followed Mama's conversation with Judee.

"I have come to end of my time," Judee said. "I wanted to see you one more time. I want to thank you for sharing my journey through life, for giving me a chance to find new home for my people."

"I thought it was you helping us," Mama replied.

"We needed your knowing how to set up new colony on new world. Back on Wat, when one group moved away, they could always go back for help. Here is just us."

"I know. We've had problems with that, too. I've always wondered, if you don't mind saying, how you got the Emprisa."

"We stole from Centar." Judee cackled as her green eyes lit up. "They thought we were trained animals."

"But you were on the Council of Five."

"Yes, as their trained animal, to always do what Jonkam wanted. Marlgar mostly did, so Jonkam only needed to get one more to do what he wanted. I got Marga to go with me if I wanted other."

"Why that so-and-so. But you fooled him, didn't you."

Judee giggled. "Also they not have mindlink receiver and we mostly converse in mind. We babble for them. Easy for some of us to learn their language."

"But their ship…"

"They build many on our moon. Had minerals they need. We have long, thin fingers," she waggled hers, "so good for working in small places and delicate things."

"Why didn't they use robots?"

"They started with ones for wiring, but too clumsy, so had to make smarter. New bots do things simpler, better, but not way Centar want. So they make them not as smart, they did what they were told. Only new Centar told one wrong, and half of ship blow up. So they said no more and found us, and our moon, bigger and better than theirs."

She paused for breath. "Our instinct is to play dumb, so we did, but learned much. Then one of my people figure out how to make ship so they not see it. Move people onboard gradually. They can't tell us apart without colors. Then when Centar leaders gone, we leave and find you."

It couldn't have been that simple, I thought, as I turned to Dela, who had all sorts of questions.

"Serves them right," Mama said. "So how are your people doing?"

"Growing. Many new young this season. But many unhappy, want to find more trees, more room."

"Same as us. More people need more room. We've got a second colony started at a river two days walk up the beach. Mostly the younger people."

I finished my telling and dropped my link to Mama.

"One of our young 'uns saw a man over by your river a while back," Dela said. "Tall and skinny, he said. But he's always seeing things.

"Oh, he saw the alien, all right. His name is Cray, and he came back with us. He lives in the forest. He won't hurt anyone."

"What is this sick you say your people have?"

I described it, and told her we three here were all over it.

Dela nodded. "So you mated. How long before offspring?"

"By winter. She's growing in here." I patted my large tummy. "You?"

"I have first daughter in pouch."

"Pouch?" I looked at her flat front.

"For infant to grow in until ready to be out. You not do it that way?"

"No. We carry ours inside until ready to live outside. About this big." I cradled my arms.

"How it come out?"

"Opening between legs."

Dela sniffed. "Hurt a lot, getting that big thing out?"

"That's what they say." I tried to image a tiny thing the size of a chick in a pouch on my front. "Aren't you afraid it'll fall out?"

"No. Always suckle at first, sticks to inside."

Before I could find out any more, Mama called us back. "It's time for us to go. I don't want you to get too tired. This is the last time we'll see Judee." She choked and turned away.

I went to Judee and touched her hand. "Thank you for all the help you gave Mama and our people," I said. "We'll miss you. I'll help Dela however I can. Go in peace."

Judee turned her now gray-green eyes to me. "Remember. Is better to fight enemy on your own home place. Live well and prosper." She closed her eyes, and I turned to Dela. "Can you get her back in the shuttle?"

"Pilot will carry her. Be safe."

Echoing her, Mama, Charley, and I left.

Chapter 34   The Second Bug

As we approached the plaza, a stab of pain in my gut knocked me to my knees. I yelped, clutched my stomach, and sat on my good side.

"No," Charley cried, grabbing me.

"What is it?" Mama demanded, dropping down beside me. "It's too soon for the baby."

"I don't know," I panted. "Not the baby." Mama helped me force the pain away. "In my gut. Not anything I ate."

A few older kids came over to see what was going on. Mama told them to go get Noa. They trotted off. "What do you think it is?" she asked me.

"No idea. I need to get home so I can really look at it." More people gathered. Noa pushed her way through. I told her what happened.

She felt around my abdomen, and looked up. "I don't feel anything except the baby, and she's fine. Do you want to come to the clinic, or go home? Are you up to walking?"

"Home." They helped me to my feet. After the dizziness faded away, I took a few steps, Charley holding me up. Noa shooed people away. Charley led me to the clinic, despite my protestations.

By the time we got there and I sat down on a bed, the pain was down to barely noticeable and I had my breathing under control. "I'm okay now."

Charley sat beside me, not letting go.

"Your heart rate is still too high," Noa said, holding my wrist. "Relax." I did some deep breathing, and after a bit, Noa added, "It's okay now. I'd like to keep you here for a while for observation."

"I really do need to go home." I struggled to my feet. Then something else hit me. "Peter," I cried. "He was hit with the same thing. I was feeling his pain too. He's at home."

"Charley, take care of her," Mama said as she trotted out.

'Does she think I don't?' I *heard* him think. "I'm taking her home. I'll let you know if anything else happens," he said to Noa, steering me to the door.

"Thanks, Noa," I added. I was able to walk normally by the time we reached the halfway point. At Mama's house, we found her ministering to Peter, curled up on his bed.

"Hey, Petey, it'll calm down in a little bit," I said, and *sent* encouragement.

"Perri, go lie down. I've got to talk to Bay and Adam," Mama said. I flopped on my bed and Charley sat in the chair as I *tuned in* as Mama described what had happened to Peter and me. Aunt Pauli joined in.

'It looks like round two,' Mama *sent*. 'Pauli, find out from Doc or Alice if this is possible, and why it's so different. Warn everyone. Let's set up a safe place for the children.'

'You and I can do that, Aunt Lyn,' Aunt Pauli *sent*.

They continued with plans as I *looked* into my body. A knot of something not of me oozed along my intestinal tract, leaving traces behind. I could not do anything to it, or even move it along faster. The traces disappeared. All I could do was wait for it to reach the end.

Mama came in to me after she was finished with the others, and I told her what I'd found. "Would you mind if I look inside you?"

"Okay." There was nothing in there that didn't belong. Mama kissed me and left me to rest. Charley sat in the chair and watched me.

I closed my eyes and tried to think. *Could they have put two different bugs in us, with different times for them to start? Or was it part of the first bug? And how many more parts or bugs were there?*

One thing was clear. I'd have to go back and find Dree and a way to get those people out of our hair. As soon as I was well again. There was still time before the baby came.

The next day, the bug dropped into the outhouse pit. I took care of the bits left behind. Peter felt better, too, after he got rid of his. I returned to my house, back to my duties, and waited to see what would happen next. If it was just in us two, no one else should get it. But if it was part two...

#

Four days later, Charley came down with it, followed by his dad and Uncle Allen. The infection went through the same path as before.

Mama and the other women who'd borne children poopooed the pain, but the men screamed. Prepuberty children only got mild stomachaches.

This time we lost more people; a few elders who had digestive system problems, a couple of men recovering from serious injuries, one gal who was just getting over food poisoning. And Aunt Alice.

Uncle Bay had sent his younger sister Aunt Maria to check on Doc and Aunt Alice, because no one had heard from them all day. She'd found Doc Richard sitting in his big chair, eyes closed, holding Aunt Alice's body against his chest.

All of us with Talent heard Maria scream, and ran to her. I limped as fast as I could. Aunt Pauli got there first, followed closely by Uncle Bay and Mama. Most were there by the time I arrived. Chad, Maria's mate, held her as she wept.

Papa and Charley, out in the fields, came later.

The Fours had automatically linked, so I was able to follow what was happening. Doc opened his red eyes and looked at us.

"She was too weak to fight it," he said. "I tried everything I could."

"I'm sure you did," Mama said, tears running down her face. "She had a long and wonderful life. We'll all miss her."

"You'll have to let her go, Uncle," Bay said, touching the old man's shoulder. "She's with the Oneness now." After Doc kissed her, Uncle Bay gently took Aunt Alice, laid her on the bed, and covered her with a sheet. He *sent* to Charley to bring Kareth and Noa.

I arrived and went to Mama. Not having seen much death, the smell shocked me. Doc and Aunt Alice had always kept themselves and their home clean. I looked around the neat, but dark, little room, and opened the curtains.

Their house held a bed, a table for two, and the two padded chairs side by side facing the large front window. Shelves on the walls held books and medical objects. A faint aroma of Aunt Alice's scent permeated the aura of loving in this room.

Maria detached herself from Chad and went to her uncle, perching on the arm of the chair, and putting an arm around him. As she laid her cheek on his head, she said, "Poor Uncle. We're all still here for you. We all love you. You'll always have her in your memories."

I felt tears running down my face. I wanted to say something, do something, but didn't know what. Uncle Art and Aunt Betty stood in a corner, alone in themselves. The children mainly milled around outside.

Finally, Aunt Pauli spoke. "Doc, when you are ready, we want you to come up and stay with us. You can have Charley's old room. We don't think you should stay here by yourself."

I knew that hurt him. He and Aunt Alice had lived there for twenty years, ever since he'd built the place himself. People murmured things, then Papa and Charley showed up, with Kareth and Noa.

"She was a wonderful woman," Noa said. "Do you want the full ceremony?"

"Yes," Mama said. "She deserves the honor." Doc stared at the small mound on the bed.

Noa pulled back the sheet. Kareth touched the face and hand. "She died in the night, yes?"

Doc nodded.

Oh my Oneness, I thought. *He's been sitting there half the night and all day with her in his lap.* I felt Charley's strong arm around me and sagged into him.

"Where do you want her?" Uncle Bay asked. "I'll carry her down."

"No," Doc muttered. "Go away. Leave me alone."

"The clinic, I think," Noa said, looking at Kareth, who nodded. Uncle Bay picked up the wrapped body and strode out the door. Kareth and Noa followed.

"Are you sure?" Mama asked Doc.

"Yes. Go."

The rest of us, except Aunt Maria, drifted out after Uncle Bay and the others. Aunt Pauli went home to prepare the room for Doc.

Uncle Adam, who'd left as soon as he had seen what the situation was, told Emek, who passed the word to his people. Those who knew Doc well passed us on their way up to pay their respects. A group of men, led by Papa, prepared the funeral barge.

That night, Charley wept in my arms. "She's always been there, her and Doc. Always willing to talk to us kids. Always watching out for us." Later, he said, "I suppose Doc won't be around much longer, either. They're both in their eighties."

"Don't say that."

"At his age, losing his life's partner, he doesn't have much to live for. He's taught everything he knows to Noa and the younger ones. He has no children. What else is there?"

"Oh, Charley, don't say that. He still has all of us to take care of." I cuddled his head.

He kissed me and turned over. I lay and thought of many things, none of which solved anything.

Chapter 35   Burial Barge

In the morning, we went by Charley's folks' house to pick up his family and Doc, who had been persuaded to go there for the night. We met Mama, Papa, and Peter on the way. Mama, red eyed and sagging, looked old.

At the clinic, Uncle Bay took up his aunt's body, now wrapped in a blanket of woven leaves. Murmuring something to her, he led the procession down the river bank to the funeral dock, where the barge awaited.

I started out near the front, but arrived near the rear. Charley and I pushed through to the dockside. All of the Terrans, Adam, and many of the Bramites were there. Uncle Bay laid the body on a raised section of the flat, oblong deck and spread out the blanket of leaves over it.

Kareth's mother, Tara, pushed to the front and stepped up on a box beside one of the poles the barge was tied to.

She spoke a paragraph in Bramish, then in Standard, our common language, and pointed to Doc. He stared at the body of his beloved.

"She was my love, my life," he began. "She took care of me in every way. She always said she didn't mind not having children, we had all of our brothers' and sisters' children. She cared about everyone, and hated what was happening to our Earth. She..." He broke down. Uncle Bay and Aunt Maria held him.

"My Aunt Alice was a wonderful woman. She was always there for us kids," Uncle Bay said. "She always reminded me of Gran, who we left behind on Earth. They were two of a kind. She was special."

He stopped, biting his lip, and Tara pointed to Mama.

"I loved her from the day we met," Mama said. "She was always willing to help, even if she didn't know how to do it. 'Just show me,' she'd say. The whole community will miss her."

Adam was next. "She reminded me of my mother," he said, blinking. "We will surely miss her."

When it was my turn, I said, "She was a wonderful woman, like a grandmother to me. We'll all miss her."

We continued through all of the Terrans, even the children, and then to the Bramites.

Emek said, "She was a pillar of the community."

Noa spoke. "She was a very wise woman," she said. "She knew how to bring the best out of all of us."

This was the Bramites' ritual, which they had used for Mama's and Papa's friends Steve and Martime, who'd died in Nubram. There, they had a lava pit. Here, we used a burial barge. Mama had decided that it was as good as anything else they could devise.

After everyone had said his or her piece, Uncle Bay and Adam lit the torches surrounding the body, untied the ropes, and pushed the barge away from the dock.

Bay jumped into a little boat and paddled around to the bow of the barge. He grabbed the front rope, tied it to his boat, and began pulling it out into the river.

"Alice," Doc cried, and dove into the water.

"No, Doc," some of us yelled. Papa and a couple others dived in after him. But Doc still had strength left in his wiry body and made it to the barge. Uncle Bay had stopped rowing and sat watching, his eyes wide.

"No," Mama and several others cried. I put my hands over my mouth. *How could he?*

We watched, horrified, as Doc pushed his way under the leaf blanket. Tiny fires dropped from one of the torches and began to burn a corner of the cover. Doc curled away from us, clutching her body.

Papa reached the barge and tried to pull Doc off, but he wouldn't budge. The craft continued to float down the river, and there was no way Bay could pull it back to shore.

I shivered, and hid my face in Charley's chest as the blanket of leaves began to burn in earnest. How *could* he, I thought again.

Out of the corner of my eye I saw Uncle Bay shrug and row farther out into the river, setting the barge free in the main current. After he dropped the rope, he turned his boat back toward us. The barge sailed on down the river into the sea. We watched the plume of smoke grow and shrink as it disappeared into the deep water.

I leaned into Charley and sent an inchoate prayer to the Oneness.

"They had full lives," Uncle Bay said, on my right.

"He always said he felt he'd come home when you all came here," Charley said. "Was it really that bad on Earth, Papa?"

"In many places," Uncle Bay said, still staring out to sea. "The hacienda was a safe haven, a place of peace. It was too far from the city for most people to bother with."

"The hacienda?" I asked.

"A large house with many rooms. My father built it. But Gran Dalia, his mother, ran it," Uncle Bay said. "All the uncles and aunts had rooms there, but most had homes elsewhere."

"Do you miss your family?" I asked. I knew they'd left a lot of people behind.

"I did at first, until I learned to visit them in my memories." Most of the people had wandered off. Charley took my arm as we followed.

"I still wonder what kind of life the twins and Bobby had," Aunt Pauli said as she came up alongside us. "My three younger sibs we left on Earth," she told me. She and I proceeded to the craft hall, while Bay and Charley went back to their duties.

Chapter 36   Cray

As life in the community settled back into its routine, an aura of sadness surrounded River Point. We Terrans, especially, felt the loss, as they had been our cousins. Most of the people who had come down from North Point stayed to help with harvest, but a few young Bramite couples trickled back up.

We'd gotten behind on a lot of things with people being sick and all. Between my growing pregnancy and my bad knee I couldn't do a lot of things I used to.

Charley wouldn't leave me unless one of our mothers was around. He would walk me down to my tasks, make sure one of the mothers was there, and go on to his own job.

One day I was complaining about it to Mama while we made up new workbooks for the children. "Charley even comes and pounds on the outhouse door if I'm in there too long."

"Men tend to be that way, especially for the first one," Mama said, placing a completed book in a pile. "And look what you've been through, Perri."

"I know, Mama, but I'm going crazy not being able to be alone for a while. And I haven't seen much of Peter lately, either. Even just going off with him would help."

"I'll tell him to find you and spend some time together. You need it."

"I also need to go up and see Cray and take him some bread. He keeps asking me when I'm going to come," I said, searching for a particular page. "He doesn't want anyone else to come with me."

"What about Peter? He was with you when you came back to Harmony."

"Yes," I said, sitting up straight. "I'll tell him I have to have an escort now because of my condition."

"I'll tell Peter tonight."

#

The next afternoon, as I finished up my class, Peter showed up swinging a bag of bread. "I'll walk her home," he said to Mama who was wrapping up her class in the other half of the room.

"Fine."

"So how's things?" Peter asked as we headed up the hill.

"Okay, except Charley won't leave me alone for a minute and I don't mean that way."

"Well you still are newlyweds," Peter smirked.

"Oh shut up."

We walked in silence for a while. "He goes out of his way to keep me away from you," Peter remarked. "I only go along with it to keep peace in the family."

"No wonder I never see you. That so-and-so." I stomped my good foot. "I've missed you, Petey, even though we connect in our minds all the time. It'll never take the place of seeing someone in person."

"I know."

"I'm aware you are uncomfortable around me in my present state, but you better get used to it. Anne will be like this next year, and neither of us are stopping at one."

"Yeah, but... He shuffled his feet and looked away.

"Ask Papa how he felt when Mama was carrying us."

"Oh."

"Come on, I want to get past our house before Charley catches up with us." I started off.

Cray had found a glade just above our cabin and met us there now. I asked him once if he minded being alone in the woods all the time.

"No, I am not alone. I can sense you, all of you, and the little brown creatures keep me company. The bread you bring is very good, too."

Somehow, he was able to tune into the Bramites better than I could, and would tell me of areas of unrest so we could take care of them.

When we arrived at the glade, Cray was there, waiting. He took a step back.

"You remember Peter," I said. "He has to escort me now." I patted my large tummy.

"Ah, yes," Cray said. We all sat down and Peter presented him with the bread. Cray thanked us. "I feel a sadness about you," he added.

"Yes, this is the first time we've lost even one of our own, let alone two." I plucked a blade of grass and played with it.

"He was a very courageous person to go like that. In Onan, when one of a pair dies, the other looks for another mate." Cray looked at Peter so he wouldn't have to look at my protruding abdomen. I'd sensed his discomfort from the time I told him I was pregnant. His people's women stayed in a compound away from the men during their pregnancies.

We discussed what was going on in our colony and in the forest. Cray noted a Bramite couple who seemed to be very unhappy together.

"I'll tell Emek," Peter said as he rose. "I think we'd better go now." He helped me up.

"Aloha," I said. "That's a word Papa taught us, from Earth. It means both 'hello' and 'goodbye'."

As we approached my house, we met Charley storming up the trail.

"Where have you been?" he yelled, pulling me into a hug.

"Peter and I went up to see Cray." I leaned into him. "I need to sit down." He led me into the house, Peter trailing behind.

I stretched out on the bed and sighed. I'd been on my feet too long. "Thanks, Petey," I said, and made a little shooing motion.

"See you," he said, and left.

I still hadn't gotten off by myself, but did have some time with Peter, soaking up all the things we had not been able to share with each other.

"What am I going to do with you?" Charley demanded. "I was so scared."

"I'm fine, honey," I said. "Women have been having babies for the last million years."

"And some die from it."

"Not me. Come here."

After that, he let me have a little more freedom, but still kept an eye on me.

A couple of tendays passed. It became harder to climb that hill to my house. Even though my knee had healed, I still had a limp. My back hurt a lot, also. Noa said that should go away after I had the baby.

Beth, Charley's sister, commiserated with me a lot; she was in the same stage of her pregnancy. As long as I was with her, he didn't worry so much about me, he worried about both of us.

Aunt Pauli kept telling him we were both fine, not that he believed it.

#

One hot day Peter and I went up to see Cray. This would be the last time for me until the baby came. After greetings and handing over some bread, Cray said, "Someone has come through the mountain gate."

"Who?" I sat up, a hand clutching at my heart.

"What," Peter exclaimed.

"I cannot tell yet. He is four or five days away. Not Dree. Prepare yourselves."

"How?" Wild thoughts scrambled through my mind.

"Hide the vulnerable, the children, inside a circle of defenders, warn others. I will *touch* you when I know more." He glanced at me, and looked away. "How is your condition?" He was still uncomfortable seeing an obviously pregnant woman running around loose by herself.

We talked a bit, and the two men helped me to my feet. "I will not be able to come up here anymore until after the baby is born," I said. "After harvest, but before cold."

"I can always reach you by mind."

"Peter will bring you bread, when you need it." I looked around the little glade not visible from any trail. I would miss this.

Chapter 37   Preparing

When we reached my house, I *called* Mama and told her what Cray had said.

'No. Not more.'

'Oh yes. If Cray says someone is up there, someone is. And they'll keep coming until they get us all.'

'Stop that. Stay there and rest. I'll get with the others.'

As I relaxed and *followed*, I *heard* her share with her Four. Uncle Adam *said* he would call a general meeting.

Since both Mama and Charley wanted me to stay home, I stayed at Mama's with Peter, and we *tuned in* through her to listen to what was going on at the gathering in the meeting hall. All of the Terrans except us, and many Bramites were there.

"People, we have a new problem," Adam said. "Perri has informed us that someone has come through the mountain Gate and will be here in a few days. Prepare to move up into the hills." He took a breath.

"Allen, you gather a crew and look for a place for a children's camp in back of the ridge. Noa, we need you and whoever can help you, to set up another clinic up in the hills. Lyn, after Allen returns, you and Pauli set up the children's camp. Figure out what you need to take over there and start collecting it. Larry, if you can, set up a second storehouse up near your cabin."

"Right," Papa said. "We also need to get as many people as possible out to harvest the early crops."

"If anyone has any other suggestions, please let Emek or me know," Adam said. "Even if it's only one person coming down, we don't know how powerful this alien is, or what weapons he may have with him. Emek, be sure all your people understand how dangerous this alien could be."

"I will make sure they do. We will keep our settlement whole," Emek said.

"If we all work together, we can meet this challenge and keep our people safe," Adam added.

As the meeting broke up, several people approached Adam. Mama disconnected us so I didn't hear what they had to say. I tried to think of what one alien could do to us against over a hundred men. It never occurred to me that someone else could have a greater mind power than I.

During the rest of the day and the next, a feeling of foreboding began to build up within me. Whatever was coming was not going to be good. I kept feeling that I should be doing more to help my people.

That evening, Cray *touched* me.

'Do you know anything more about the alien that came through the Gate?' I asked.

'It is Brasca, a terminator. The Gatekeepers send it to worlds where they want the natives exterminated. I cannot tell yet what weapons it may have.'

'What does it look like?' I asked.

'It is man-like, larger than I am, but not alive in the way you and I are. It is usually gray, with orange glowing eyes.'

Cray sighed. 'You have the advantage of knowing beforehand. Get everyone out of your village that you can. Send as many as possible to your northern settlement. Make a secret place in the forest for your children and anyone else who cannot fight.'

I shivered. *There must be something we could do, there was only one of him.* But we had no weapons as such; we'd never needed them.

'I will keep contact with you so you can follow Brasca's progress. He is not infallible. May your people survive and live in peace.'

'Thank you,' I *sent*. Immediately I *reached* to Mama and told her what Cray had said. We both prayed to Oneness to help our people.

As Mama told the rest of her Four, I *reached* to the others in my Four. Their reactions ranged from alarm to grim determination to beat this alien.

Charley came running home and grabbed me in his arms. "You're staying up here," he said, squeezing the breath out of me. "I've volunteered to work on the clinic."

"Okay," I said, when he released me and I could breathe.

"How long before this thing gets here?" he asked.

"Cray said about four days." I sat down on the side of the bed. The chairs were too hard for me now, and Charley brought one to face me.

"Our first concern must be you and the baby," he began. "I want you as far away from that thing as possible." He must have read my mind, because he added, "No, I'm not sending you up to North Point. That's too far for you to walk."

"I have to stay here," I said. "I have to be close enough to deal with the alien if I have to."

"We'll have plenty of people down there to deal with him."

"I know, but he must have something he thinks he can use on all of us before we can get him down." I tugged a curl. "And the idea of something that powerful scares me silly."

Charley took my hands. "Let's hope it has something to do with sound, then you won't be able to hear it, if you shut down your link to the rest of us."

"Okay."

"But right now," he pulled me to my feet, "It's been a long day and I'm starving."

#

In the morning, Charley took me down to Mama's and went on to start collecting tools and supplies for the new clinic. "What do you want me to do?" I asked Mama.

"First, let's start here and see what we can donate to the new children's camp," she said. Together we packed two large baskets with blankets, cloths, old clothes and toys Peter and I had outgrown, and a few extra mugs and dishes.

Uncle Allen came by with several other young men. "We're going over the ridge to find a place for the children," he said. "We would like to know if you have any particular requirements."

"Um," Mama said, thinking. "First of all it needs to be in a large open space well sheltered by trees, with no underbrush. We'll want space for enough dorms and smaller residences, a large gathering room, and a kitchen and laundry house, with a stream or springs nearby for water. And a downhill area to one side for the latrine."

"Okay," Uncle Allen said, repeating her instructions. "We'll be back late tomorrow and let you know what we find."

"Thank you," Mama said.

"Also," Uncle Allen continued, "Han is rounding up families to take up to North Point tomorrow. The day after tomorrow I'm going to take as many young people as I can down south. Emek is working on his people to move up into the hills for a few days, and he and Adam have sent a few men up to the top of the trail."

"Very good," Mama said. "Good luck."

"See you tomorrow," Uncle Allen said, and his group took off up the trail.

"Let's go see Pauli," Mama told me. We went over to Aunt Pauli's house and helped her pack up a couple more baskets. After that, Aunt Pauli went down to help with sorting out the storehouse, and Mama and I went around to other houses to help people sort and pack stuff. We made sure that families with children packed their favorite toys.

That night, Cray *told* me we had two more days, and Brasca should show up the day after that.

'Early, late?'

'Late. Means still unknown, but could be mental. Keep shut down, all of you with Talent.'

'Thanks.' I shivered. The foreboding grew stronger, coalescing into a dark cloud. What could we do to dispel it?

I *reached* and sensed a being in the far distance, but there were no details. Terror enveloped me, and I had to claw my way out. We'd never had any real problems other than the weather. I was at a loss, and so was most everyone else.

Chapter 38   Brasca

In the morning, when Charley brought me to her house, Mama told me that Uncle Allen had contacted her. "He wants me and whoever else is going to run the children's camp to gather up some children and follow the trail. He says he's found a really good place," she said. "So I want you to go to your house, pack up whatever you need, and we'll pick you up."

"Mama, I have to stay here. I've got the strongest Talent."

"Over my dead body. You'll be able to reach him from there, with the Fours."

"And mine," Charley added. "Remember our baby." He kissed me and went off to his tasks.

Mama linked with Aunt Pauli and gathered the other Terran women and children together. We took Charley and Beth's younger sisters and brother, and the others fifteen or younger. Gabe was up at North Point, and Adam had told him to stay there.

Maria and Kareth would come the next day with as many as they could round up.

"Mama, we need to shut down our Talent," I said. "Cray told me he thought the alien had mental ability." We did, all but a tenuous link of Fours, and with Uncle Allen.

We started out. The trail Uncle Allen made for us was easy to follow. When we arrived, we found that the children's camp had been laid out. Uncle Allen and the other fellows were already working on some of the buildings. Mama and Papa, and the others of their generation had their little one-room cottage laid out, and I had one as well.

I looked around. This place was a cozy little valley with a stream running through it, and dotted with tall and wide umbrella trees. A few patches of little yellow flowers flourished here and there. It was warmer here without the sea breeze.

We began to get settled, and I *checked* on the alien every so often. Late in the afternoon, Charley showed up with Noa, Karil, their children, except Nell who was up at North Point with her mate, and several Bramite women with their children.

"Uncle Allen is on his way south with a large group," Charley told us. "Emek is getting his people up in the hills, and the rest of the children will come over tomorrow."

Noa took Mama and me aside. "I'm going back to the new clinic tomorrow. We've got a couple of women who are ready to birth any time. Lila and your Beth. I just want to see where my children will be, and that they'll be all right."

"Yes," Mama said. She and I both felt Noa's continued delight in finally being able to have children after they moved out of the cavern on Brama.

We helped people settle in, and Charley went to work on the gathering hall. The other guys had put together a rudimentary kitchen and were erecting walls around the long dorm. I wandered around looking for a place to sit down.

Someone found a newly built stool, and I sank down on it with gratitude. I watched everyone bustling around, Mama at the kitchen, and wished I could help.

After a hastily scrabbled together supper, Charley rigged up a hammock for me. Every else slept on the ground.

The next day, Chad and Maria and a group of Bramites showed up about midmorning.

After getting them settled, I *touched* Beth. She had a healthy little boy.

#

Late afternoon of the second day, I received a brief message from Cray. 'Brasca is at top of trail. I'll be watching.' I told Mama, and she *sent* a message to Adam, to go house to house to make sure everyone had left.

All the rest of the day, people with children poured into camp. Charley and Art Junior shepherded anyone who could work on construction to the areas where building was proceeding. Mama and Aunt Pauli showed the women and children to their temporary homes. Aunt Maria and I collected the food and supplies they'd brought, and we had the younger girls take them to the kitchen and the storehouse area.

Via Adam's link, we were aware that a group of about a dozen families refused to leave. They said it was too far, all Terran nonsense, a trick to get their houses. "What can one man do against all of us, anyway?" one fellow asked.

"It is your life, and your death," Emek said. "Sleep well. It may be your last."

"Idiots," Mama said.

"It's not fair to the kids," I added. "Don't they care about their children?"

"I guess not." Mama shook her head and turned back to her cooking. We set out food here and there on makeshift tables and people ate as they could take time out from their duties.

Fortunately, it was the time of year when the days were longest, and the builders worked until they could no longer see.

We all dropped onto our sleeping blankets in exhaustion. Charley promised me he'd build me a sleeping platform the next day.

When I checked on the alien in the morning, he was up near the first campsite above the trail. Later, Cray *told* me he still couldn't detect a physical weapon, so he was pretty sure it was mental.

I spread the word, and we let Adam know. He and Emek were hanging out in the plaza, and Peter was over there somewhere, too, in spite of Mama's pleas.

We continued our work, and Mama stayed linked with Adam. When I *found* the alien at the top of the trail, I quit checking. I didn't want him to notice me.

After the midday meal, Mama told us the alien was approaching the plaza. I *tuned in* and learned that Adam and Emek had stationed themselves in the center of the open area surrounded by the community buildings.

We Fours followed them through Adam's link. Mama went around telling everyone we were safe back there. I sensed a growing fear and apprehension in the population. I also began to *sense* the alien in detail, and followed Brasca as he moved down the trail.

Although not much taller, he was a lot bigger than Cray, and dressed in the same sort of clothing, all gray. Brasca carried a bag like Cray's, and the black cloud of danger almost strangled me. There was something strange in his mind I couldn't figure out. The only thought I could get was of doing his duty. The alien only stopped when he reached the center of the plaza.

Brasca spoke. We not only heard him via Adam, but the others, Terrans and Bramites alike, heard his voice. Mama told me later that even Papa had heard it.

"You will follow me to Gate."

I shivered. How could he make us? I felt a bit of a tug from the Gate, and the black cloud squeezed me.

"No," Mama said, clutching me and Papa. She'd felt the cloud too.

"No," Adam and Emek said together. "You will not take our people. This is our home and we intend to keep it," Adam added. "Who are you, and why do you want us gone?" I *sensed* Adam's determination and Emek's unease.

Brasca huffed out a small breath, took a step forward, and repeated its statement. Adam and Emek stepped back and sideways toward the hill.

"Do as I say." Brasca took another step.

"Not 'til you tell us who you are and why."

Brasca stared straight ahead.

"He doesn't know how to respond," Adam said to Emek.

"How do you know?" Emek demanded. "Have you seen this thing before?"

"No," Adam said, looking around.

We saw through Adam's eyes that a couple of older Bramites were approaching the plaza. Emek shouted a Bramish word I didn't know, and added, "Go home now. Go back now."

The couple stopped, looked at him, then at Brasca.

"Go, go, in the name of Bram, go," Emek pleaded. They looked at him, the man shook his head a little, and they moved to Brasca's side.

"You will come with me," Brasca said, and looked around. The alien repeated its first statement. More people appeared and joined it. Emek shouted himself hoarse to no avail.

"We cannot stop him," Adam said, leading Emek up the hill into the trees. Even we Fours could not break its spell. As more Bramites came, Adam marched on up the hill. Emek ran back, grabbed the arm of a motherly woman, but she shook him off.

Brasca looked at him, said, "Come with us."

Emek turned and ran up the hill. "They're taking my people and you do nothing," he panted as he caught up with Adam.

"Lyn's people are doing everything they can. This being is stronger somehow. He is taking them to the beach Gate. We must prepare a defense there. We must gather people and take the shortcut through the forest." Adam strode on up the trail.

Chapter 39   Betty

At the children's compound, Bay said, "The alien is going downriver to the beach." Several of us were meeting in the gathering place, an open sided structure with a roof of branches and leaves, to discuss our options.

"To the Gate," I said. "The alien will take them there and send them through." I was positive of this.

"Will it be to where you went?" Mama asked.

I looked at Peter who had returned to camp. He shrugged. "Could be," I said. "Or not. If they can set the Gates to go anywhere... I don't know."

Uncle Bay stood up in his corner. "Let's grab some supplies and head up the shortcut to the Gate. Maybe we can stop them there."

Most of the men and some of the women, including Mama, quickly packed up provisions and took off. Charley and Mama didn't want me to go, but I wasn't going to be left out. After they'd all gone, I slipped out after them. I could sense where they were, and followed as fast as I could. I kept my link to Charley low, so that he wouldn't notice it.

Warm even in the shade of the trees, I stopped and wiped my face. I'd not been this way before. They'd planned it while I was gone. Although it was safe here, the silence overwhelmed me. Only my link with Charley kept me going, even though he got farther and farther ahead.

As I moved on, I heard him. 'Perri, where are you?'

I kept quiet. I didn't want him to send me back. Both scared and excited, I limped on. Focusing on the alien, I saw that he and the people with him had reached the beach. How could I, we, ever stop him? His link was totally different than mine.

Suddenly, Charley ran out of the trees and grabbed me. The forest came alive with noise. "What are you doing out here by yourself?" he demanded.

"I told you I wasn't going to stay back there."

"But you can't hear if something sneaks up on you."

"And I can't hear that alien calling to me, either. How are you doing with it?"

"I have a block on it, like everyone else. One of us is always close to Betty and Papa Larry. Now come on." He tried to pick me up, set me down. "Boy, you weigh a ton."

"I've gained a little weight in the last few months, in case you haven't noticed," I snapped.

"I have. Hold on." Charley said. He put my arm up to his shoulder, wrapped his arm around my waist, and took off, swinging me along at a faster pace than I could walk by myself.

"Hey," I yelped.

"Hang on. You're going for a ride."

I half strangled him, but it didn't slow him down. After a short time, we caught up with the rest, and he handed me to Papa. The men traded off carrying me, and we moved faster than I thought possible, Mama and Aunt Betty puffing along in the rear.

The setting sun glared at us when we reached the beach. "They're a little more than halfway here," I reported. Charley, who'd been carrying me, put me down.

"They're walking in the soft sand," Uncle Bay said. "No wonder."

"Dummies," Peter snorted.

"Maybe they don't have beaches on their world," Mama added.

"Cray said they do, but this guy probably never went to one," I said, stretching.

"You guys catch your breath, and start on a barricade," Mama said, "and we gals will set up camp. Who brought food?"

The men dragged downed trees and branches out of the forest and set them up across the beach below the rock.

We women unpacked and set up camp. Once I sat back and relaxed, I felt the pull of the Gate, even with my Talent practically shut down. I kept enough of a connection with Mama and Charley so I could hear what was going on.

"In the water, too," Papa puffed, dragging a big branch out into the sea. We women pitched in, planting sharp pointed sticks facing south in the tangle of branches.

Somehow, I didn't think it would stop the alien.

From my link with Adam, I knew that he had told Gabe to keep everyone up in North Point; that Aunt Pauli and the girls were keeping a clamp on the children at their compound; and that Uncle Allen and his group were just now looking for a place to camp, well south of River Point. Uncle Bay had disappeared into the forest, away from our mob.

"Look," Aunt Betty said, pointing. A pale glow flickered far down the beach.

"Here they come," I said. There seemed to be more Bramites than before. Emek pushed past me and ran toward them.

"Come back," Adam yelled, starting after him. Charley and Papa followed. As they closed in on the other group, Charley dived at Emek and pulled him down.

"Nice tackle," Papa said. The three pulled a fighting Emek to the side and held him as the group passed.

"I have to save my people," Emek yelled.

Brasca stopped at the barrier. The Bramites with him milled around. For a moment, I thought we had stopped him.

Slowly, the alien began to turn to his right, away from the sea. We all watched as his turning took him around to face the sea. He began to walk toward the rock, the others following.

I had to do something. I shut down my links and limped up to the terminator and yelled in its face, "Stop!" It tried to move around me but I moved in front of it. The silence was eerie.

Brasca said something, but I couldn't hear what it said. The people around him moved restlessly. I pounded on its chest, harder than Charley's, but not metal, and yelled. "Stop it, stop it."

He pushed me away and continued on.

Charley grabbed me and pulled me away. When we were far enough up the beach, we linked.

"What do you think you were doing?" he demanded.

"Trying to stop him. Trying to save the people." I was frustrated and scared. There must be some way to stop that monster.

The people went in up to their knees, hips, waist. A storm in the west sent waves slapping at them. One woman fell, then another. Those who'd saved the people on the beach went in after them and pulled them out. The rest marched up the rock and into the mist.

I cried because there was nothing I could do to stop them. Brasca stood and watched.

Then, disaster. Aunt Betty, helping another woman, could not move fast enough when Brasca turned and looked at her. She dropped the woman with a splash and started toward him.

"No, Betty," Art screamed, dashing toward her. Brasca took her arm and marched her up the rock. Uncle Art splashed after, but couldn't catch them. As I stared at the flickering where she'd disappeared, Uncle Art collapsed on the rock.

I was so furious, I ran out to the alien. A clear shield came down over the alien's face, but it did not cover the earholes on the side of his head.

I reached up with my right hand and slapped the left side of his head as hard as I could. He shook his head and the line of people stopped. My family started grabbing Bramites and pulling them back up the beach.

Brasca's lips began to move and the people started to walk toward the rock again. Mama and Charley grabbed Papa and pulled him back up the beach.

I hit the monster again, and again, the people stopped, briefly

"That's it," I said aloud. This time I boxed him on both earholes. His head fell forward as the Bramites stopped.

Charley let go of Papa as they charged down into the water to rescue the Bramites.

I backed away from the alien, into Mama's arms. Only then did I think of Joan. To lose her mother… I *sent* her a huge, loving hug.

After Emek gathered his people into a group, Charley and Papa came over to us and the Fours wrapped me in them.

"Now I understand why you were born deaf," Mama said, hugging me. When we broke up, I saw Brasca still standing there, his chin on his chest.

"It doesn't know what to do," Papa said. "It has no instructions for this event

He and Charley turned it to face the rock and gave it a push.

"Go to rock," Papa said.

Brasca began to walk toward the rock. With Papa and Charley giving an occasional push, he splashed out to the rock and stopped. Papa lifted on of the alien's legs and put the foot on the first step. Both men heaved the alien up to the step. They repeated this for the second step. At the third step, the alien began to climb by itself. Charley followed it up, giving the alien a little push whenever it slowed down.

At the top, one last shove, and Brasca walked into the mist and disappeared.

Mama took me up to the campsite, where we sat on makeshift benches, and rest of the Terrans and Adam gathered around.

"So that's one for Perri," Peter said, appearing from out of the forest. "Good going, sis."

"Thanks." All I wanted to do was curl up in Charley's arms and block out the world. This was only one. I knew there would be more.

My baby kicked and I grabbed my stomach. Mama moved to my side. "She moved," I said. For the first time, she was physically real.

Larry and Charley brought Emek back from where he had collapsed, and Kareth took him up to the camp. He curled like a baby in her arms. I *felt* his despair; he'd failed his people, he was no longer worthy to be a son of Bram.

"We saved ten of them," Mama said. "But Betty…"

"I know." I watched Uncle Art's cousins Bay and Chad go out to him and bring him back to shore. His white-faced son, Junior, met him, and the two walked arm in arm up the beach. I *felt* their anguish.

His kids, I thought. How to tell them? Then I realized that Aunt Pauli knew what happened and would be with them.

"He, or someone like him, will be back," Papa said. "We need to build a barricade around the rock."

"With a hidden way through." I leaned on Charley.

"No," Mama said, taking my arm.

"Mama," I said, and stopped. No point in bringing it up now.

Adam came to us. "All the other groups are all right," he said.

"Thank Oneness for that," Mama said. "Let's go eat."

No one was very hungry, and Bay and his cousins had taken Uncle Art and Junior off away from the rest of us.

"I couldn't stop her, I couldn't get to her," Uncle Art muttered over and over.

I prayed that Brasca had taken her somewhere where she could live a decent life, and maybe I could find her someday.

Chapter 40   Aftermath

No one slept much that night. I had nightmares about being chased through Gates, and I suspected others had their own variety of bad dreams. Charley woke me up once, twitching in his sleep.

In the morning, we found no signs of any aliens and decided it was safe to bring people back from North Point and for Allen to return with his group.

Adam left for River Point with Emek as soon as they had grabbed a bite to eat.

The people up at North Point were in no hurry to come down. "They'll come back when they get hungry," Papa said.

We packed up, and most of us took the inland trail to the children's compound. Papa and a few others stayed, to start working on the barrier around the rock.

At the camp, Uncle Art gathered his children and left. The rest of us comforted the Bramites on their losses, and began to pack up. Slowly, in groups, people began to head back to River Point.

Charley took me over to our house. On the way, I couldn't help but think of the people we'd lost, about twenty, I thought. "Twenty people I let die," I mumbled.

"Perri, stop that," Charley said. "You're good, but there's still lots you can't do. Don't blame yourself. You did what you could." He hugged me.

I still couldn't stop thinking that there must have been something else I could have done.

A sense of sadness permeated the community. People plodded along about their tasks. There were no songs, no laughter, no joy.

I could not concentrate on anything, and one day, found Adam and Papa discussing the future of our colony. I listened in for a while, couldn't think of anything to contribute, and wandered off.

Marisa was taking more of my attention now. I had to order a cradle from the woodcarvers, and start to collect baby clothes.

#

The day after everyone returned, we held a mass ceremony, with a small token barge, to honor the missing. Relations donated small belongings, a special cup, a piece of clothing, an object the missing one had created. These things were arranged on the barge, and a gray cloth laid over them inside a circle of torches.

Beginning with Tara, everyone spoke about the missing. The torches were lit, and Bay in his little boat pulled the barge out into the river. We watched the craft sail down the river to the sea.

Uncle Art stood with us but did not speak, a blank, empty shell. He had shut his Talent down.

Afterward, he moved into his lab, with Art Junior as his aide. Junior built on extra rooms to his own house and moved his younger siblings in with his family.

Adam and a still shaken Emek had to adjust schedules again, and promote several young people to their missing parents' positions. Some of them were not quite ready for these responsibilies, which created more problems.

Crops ripened, and were harvested haphazardly. Mama wouldn't let me go out into the fields to work, although she did. Those who'd stayed in North Point were called back to help.

A late summer storm blustered through. The rain and wind kept us indoors, where we caught up with mending, basket weaving, and such. Afterward, the trails were muddy and buried in twigs and leaves. Although the blow did no major damage, we had to spend more time cleaning up.

The storm also slowed the harvest even more.

Emek and Karil oversaw the shuffling of housing; some survivors moved in to their late parents' houses, while others brought their folks' stuff to their homes. Still others switched around.

Charley moved us down to Doc and Alice's house, much closer to the center and the clinic.

At night, in bed, sometimes I could sense their presence. I still missed Doc and Alice, but was thankful they hadn't been caught up in this last mess. I battled with a sense of frustration overlaid with sadness. One fourth of the original generation was gone.

Gan, Emek's eldest son, and Gabe spent a lot of time with their fathers, and Mama went over everything she did for the community with me. I fought the idea that my generation was going to be taking over soon, even though I knew rebelling was a losing proposition.

Some of the men were building defenses, around the rock and at the top of the trail. They were also building another path that led west, disguising our trail. We could do that, and keep a watch with our Talents, but that wasn't enough. Not if we couldn't *touch* or *reach* them.

I spent a lot of time thinking about this threat, and the only thing I could come up with was relying on our adaptability. I still wanted to confront them face to face, but I knew now I would have to wait until after Marisa came. And after... I didn't want to give up nursing her to a wet nurse, but that would be two more years or so. And by then, there would be another baby on the way.

Chapter 41   Harvest Feast

One day I *asked* Cray if he could go back to his world and find out what they were doing, but he refused.

'If I went back, they would either send me to another world where I might or might not survive, or get rid of me. What I was before, is gone. The first time I said or did anything, they'd know I was there, and where I was. I cannot hide from them. Even Dree would be required to notify them.'

Before I could say anything, he added, 'If you try to go back, they will know you at once, and either gate you to another world or send you back here with something in you that will kill everyone.'

I knew that was true, and I couldn't go for a while anyway. 'So how can we defend against them?' I told him what we were doing at the rock and the top of the trail.

'Good. Also they are afraid of heights. I feel it when one of them gets close to window high up. If you clear cliff side of trail so they can see down, might help.'

I nodded. 'We'll do that.' I *felt* Cray shudder and twitch. 'Are you all right?'

'No, but don't worry, little one. What will be, will be.' He sighed. 'It has been good, here.'

No, I thought. I *felt* it, he was dying. *I can't handle this.* 'Is there anything I, we, can do?'

'Just bring bread when you can.'

'I won't be able to come up there for a while, but I'll send Peter.'

'Farewell.' I sensed Cray moving away into the woods.

He was a friend, even though he came from a different culture. In my mind I couldn't see the trees, just a tall, thin man in brown walking away.

I heaved myself up off the couch and limped over to the table. Things were changing much too quickly. Marisa kicked in agreement. She was growing awfully fast, but Noa hadn't found any problems.

I wasn't sure of my due date, because of our time on the other worlds, but it didn't seem as if it should be this soon.

When I thought of what Cray had told me, several things came together. His people were afraid of heights. Judee saying conquer from home ground, and her people lived in trees. And Doc saying people who fight for their land and their lives, fight a lot harder than invaders.

When Mama arrived at my house, I was waiting. I poured out my thoughts. "Not just up in the forest, but actually up in the trees."

"They could probably still sense us up there, and we can't take anyone away from the harvest right now," she said. "But it's a good idea. I'll tell Adam and Bay about the heights thing."

As the trail group came back down, they cleared as much brush as possible along the dropoff side. All these little things, but what could we do to put a final stop to this? I thought about everything a lot as I prepared vegetables for winter storage.

One day Peter asked, "What if they never come back?"

"They will," I said. "They know they didn't get us all."

#

A few days later, Mama and I received a message from Judee. 'It is time,' she *sent*. 'The Oneness calls.'

"No," I cried. Mama clutched my arm.

'You will know. Live well and prosper.'

We sat stunned, staring at each other. We *sensed* Judee lifting to the sky, taking the shuttle to the Emprisa.

"No," Mama cried, jerked to her feet. We could only wait as the great ship came to life one last time. Outside, we watched her sail overhead, to the east. On the far side of Harmony we *felt* Judee let go and the Emprisa crash into the far sea. Somehow I knew she was safe with the Oneness. I held Mama as she wept. Our world grew another hole.

#

By the time of Harvest Feast, we had heard or seen no sign of the aliens. I was glad of that, but something inside told me they would be back, sooner or later. And they would have something far worse to use on us.

Always before, everyone, except for the women looking after the children, had worked in the fields, gathering everything they could. The river flooded over there every few years, so we had good soil.

This year we had a lot fewer people, even with the North Pointers back down, and the crops were smaller than previous years. It would be a lean winter.

When I mentioned this to Mama, she said, "Not as bad as our first winter on Harmony. The only thing we had a lot of, after Bay showed the guys how to build a boat, was fish. We survived then, and we'll survive this time."

Some days later we began preparing for Harvest Feast. It wouldn't be as abundant as last year. I longed to be in the middle of everything, but was forced to mainly sit and watch the men dig fire pits and put together tables and benches. As I grew heavier, my knee protested more. I willingly did whatever little tasks the women gave me.

I was also focused on the impending arrival of my child. She was making it very clear that she wanted to come out and see the world for herself. Mama and Noa kept a close eye on me.

Peter rarely came around. He was terrified about being around birthing, and also of what he might feel through our link. I'd told him I'd shut down, but I don't think he could accept that.

One morning I saw him and yelled, "Hey Petey." He looked at me from the other side of the big serving table. "I'm fine. Come here."

He trotted over. "You know, sometimes I can *sense* her," he said, moving behind me to rub my shoulders.

"Through our link?"

"Yeah."

"So what are you up to?"

"Looking for Han. He's taking Charley and me fishing."

"You in a boat?" I leaned back against him. "Don't fall asleep."

"Charley wanted me to keep him company. He said we need to learn how to fish, for our future families. Gotta go." He gave me a quick kiss and trotted off.

"You guys be careful," I called after him. Now I had them both to worry about.

Charley came by to tell me about the fishing trip. "Han says the sea is unusually quiet this morning. We're not going out that far."

"Okay," I said as he leaned over and gave me a hug. "Can you please keep Peter out of trouble this time?"

Charley flushed and walked away. "Charley," I said to his back. He didn't stop.

Me and my big mouth. *Please, Oneness, don't let anything happen to them.*

Marisa stirred within me. "Not yet," I said to her. "Not 'til after the feast." She kicked me, and settled down. Several women came over with armloads of large loovah leaves to line the firepits. A sudden yearning to be over there picking leaves washed over me. *Next year,* I thought. Or was it me?

Mama bustled here and there and everywhere. She and Kareth were in charge of food preparation. Some people were rounding up chickens to be beheaded, plucked, and cooked. I finished cutting root vegetables and took them to the main work table.

As I continued on to the outhouse, a strange feeling came over me, as if some part of me was suddenly missing. Holding onto a seat back, I checked. Baby and everyone else were fine. Except... "No," I cried out. "Cray, no." But he was gone. No sign of him anywhere. My bladder urged me on.

Aunt Pauli appeared. "Are you okay?"

"Outhouse," I said, trying to assimilate the shock. She took my arm and helped me there. By the time I came out, things had settled down, around a large hole in myself. I'd never realized how important he'd been to me.

"I'm okay," I told Aunt Pauli as she escorted me back to my seat. If it had been Mama with me, I'd have told her. But not Aunt Pauli. She'd never liked the idea of an alien hanging around in the woods outside the settlement.

Mama showed up a short time later. "What happened?"

"Cray's gone. Mama, too many things are happening, I can't handle it all. What am I going to do?"

She pulled me into a hug. "Your baby will be here soon, and afterwards you can have a nice long rest. Try not to worry about the aliens, the rest of us will do that. Enjoy the feast and the birth of your firstborn. You know that Noa and Charley and I will always be here for you." She rubbed my back.

"Thanks, Mama. Have Peter and Charley come back yet?" I asked. I needed Charley's arms around me.

"I haven't seen them. Just a minute. They're on the way up river, they'll be here soon. How is she doing?" She looked at my tummy.

"She wants to come out and play. I told her to wait 'til after the feast. Is it too soon?"

"Well, it's only been seven months here, but you spent longer away than we had here. Larry could figure it out. But if she's ready, she should be okay."

After the guys showed up with a net full of smelly fish, Charley took me over to the clinic. Noa looked me over.

"Not much longer," she said.

"I know. She wants to come out real badly."

Noa was one of the few Bramites who understood about our Talents and accepted them. "She may not wait. She's already about as low as she can get. Try to get some sleep." She led me to one of the clinic beds.

I slept fitfully, with dreams of being chased by invaders with the baby hanging halfway out. When I did wake up, to a contraction, I was filled with mixed feelings. Pleasure and relief that Marisa would arrive that day. My excitement about the feast, tempered with disappointment that I wouldn't be able to enjoy it as much as I'd have liked. And that black cloud of danger hanging over us.

Chapter 42   Aliens and Baby Coming

I sat on the bed in the clinic room with splotchy blue walls surrounding me on three sides, the tan curtain pulled across the opening and *reached*.

"Oh, no," I cried, hugging my tummy. A group of Cray's people and others milled around at the top of the trail. My first thought was, *not now*. The black cloud deepened about me.

I wanted to run and hide, but I was physically unable to run, and I couldn't hide from Mama and the others. No, you must face it, I told myself. Taking a deep breath, I *called* Mama and the Fours.

"Oh, buggers," Mama said. "Not now. We'll keep an eye on them. You take care of yourself and the baby."

Uncle Allen and a few other hefty guys went up the trail to reconnoiter. He *told* us that there were six people and two beings inside square red carts that ran by themselves.

I recognized the leader as Dree. He was looking for Cray. If we could just keep them away for the day, I thought.

"Oneness, help me," I said aloud. "Help all of us." I felt very uncomfortable inside, in between occasional contractions, and could hardly move my heavy body. How could I deal with these people?

Noa stuck her head into my room. "Oh, you're up. Have you been…" I nodded.

"Noa, we've got bigger problems. Eight aliens are on the upper trail."

"Oh, no. What can we do?" She made a fist.

"I need to get up in the hills before Marisa comes."

"Yes. You're much too vulnerable here. But your house is too far away."

"No, we're in Doc's house now. I can manage that."

Mama stomped in. "I told them to leave the guards up there until this morning, but Adam let them come down yesterday for the feast. Now look what happened," Mama fumed.

"What could they have done?" Noa asked.

"At least given us warning. Set traps. I don't know, but Allen could have done something. Perri, we need to get you out of here."

"Yes, to new clinic," Noa said, helping me to my feet and to a seat outside.

"I want to stay here for the feast," I protested. "When the aliens get close, then I'll go up there."

"We'll see," Mama said as she and Noa left. The medic returned with a nutritional drink, and Kareth brought me a pile of cloths to fold as napkins. Charley sat with me for a few minutes before Uncle Allen and Gabe hauled him off to do something.

Every time I had a contraction, I said, "Not yet, sweetie."

Adam and Emek lit the fires in the cooking pits. Women wrapped chicken and fishes in loovah leaves and laid them in the pits. Kareth and others brought bowls of vegetables. Children ran everywhere with their new toys; dolls, animals, boats, carved by the older men.

Mama kept an eye on the aliens. She reported that they were at the top of the trail, the carts stopped. A couple of Dree's men were checking out the fake trail. I sat and *watched* and trembled inside. We couldn't keep them away forever.

I saw Mama talking to Adam, and wondered what that was about. Inside, Marisa was very quiet, just biding her time. I felt like I was in a place where time had stopped.

Breads and sweetmeats and fruits filled bowls at one end of the serving table, piles of dishes sat on a side table. Most of the colonists were milling around, awaiting the food.

Adam looked around, found Emek, and they and Mama stepped up on a low stage at the side of the plaza.

"Welcome to the Harvest Feast," Emek said. "Adam has an announcement."

Adam stepped forward. I heard them through Mama. "People, I have bad news. We have discovered that there are more aliens coming from up above the head of the trail."

The crowd murmured, some angrily. "First, we need people to take the children over the ridge to the camp there, right now."

"Yes," I whispered, "get the children out of here."

Someone yelled, "How much time do we have?"

"At least a couple of hours, maybe more, depending how long we can hold them there," Adam said.

Mama touched his shoulder. He moved aside and let her speak.

"Women and girls, start packing up what food and supplies you can carry," she began. "Eat as you work. Those of you who live nearest the top of the trail, go to your homes now to collect what you can and return to the plaza. Those who live nearby, collect food and supplies here, then go to your homes, collect what you can, and go on over to the camp."

She stopped, closed her eyes, took a breath. I *sent* her a hug.

"Men and boys," she continued. "Leave the tables as they are. Choose some of you to stay until the chickens and fishes are cooked, then the boys can pack them up and bring them to the camp. The rest of you can pack supplies. We will need people to go around and make sure everyone is accounted for." She looked around with bleak eyes.

I heaved myself to my feet. "We will survive," I yelled, as the words also came out of Mama's mouth. We looked at each other across the plaza and made a new connection. I became part of the First Four, now Five. The other four surrounded me mentally, and I knew we would survive.

I was filled with a sense of wonderment, of being beyond this mundane world, of being more than mere human. And then the feeling was gone, and I was only a woman with Talent, a woman about to produce a child.

Adam dismissed the crowd with a "Let's go, people."

Mama made her way across to me, followed by Peter and Charley. Noa, nearby, joined us. Aunt Pauli arrived with a platter of food piled helter-skelter. It smelled wonderful, but I didn't think I could eat anything. However, I tasted a bit of squash, Aunt Maria's special bread, and a sweet pudding.

"Uh oh," Mama said. "They've caught on and are back on the real trail. But going single file."

After the others finished gobbling their food, they left the plates on the table, and stood.

Mama said, "We've got to get Perri out of here now, to the new clinic. That's as far as she can go. Noa's got the birthing chair up there."

Papa and Charley began hustling me away toward our trail. "Now?" Charley squeaked. I realized he was definitely not ready for the arrival of his daughter.

"Oh," I yelped, as something tricked down my leg. "My water just broke." Noa caught up with us. "Oh," I repeated, as a contraction bent me forward. "Not yet, baby. Not now." In the back of my mind I was aware of people running around like disturbed ants.

Chapter 43   Birth and Death

I got as far as our new house and could go no farther. Noa told Charley to run up to the new clinic and get the birthing chair. Peter went with him. I curled up on the bed and waited.

Mama and I linked with Adam. He and Emek were the only ones left in the plaza. They'd extinguished the fires in the fire pits and tidied up what they could, as they waited for whatever would come.

In between contractions, I tried to focus on Dree as he and the others reached the top of the settlement. I could *sense* his emotions and strong thoughts. The group of aliens took the river road, checking each house as they passed. Once I *felt* the cart beings, which I supposed were gatekeepers, communicating with Dree, although I couldn't tell what was said, except that it was a command.

They found one older couple sitting at their table eating. After communication from a gatekeeper, Dree said something to the couple. When they refused to leave, some kind of energy came out of the cart and the couple disappeared.

"No," I moaned. Noa thought it was a contraction.

Two of Dree's men grabbed the plates and gobbled down the rest of the food, although Dree tried to stop them.

I *reached* and caused the food to be poisonous to them. Three houses later, the two were left curled up and groaning on the ground. Some of our men there pulled them into the woods and tied them up.

"Two down and six to go," I muttered. I could feel Marisa pushing at me to get out. My mind was divided. The main part was focused on Marisa and her impending arrival, but a small area remained linked with Adam.

Adam watched as the group approached. Dree moved out in front as they stopped. The two males stared at each other.

"What do you want?" Adam asked.

"Where are your people?"

Dree's three fellows ran to the serving table to gobble up the food, even though Dree yelled 'no'.

After I caught my breath from a contraction, I made them sick, too. The three soon curled up, moaning. Adam and Emek stood and watched.

At the house, Charley and Peter arrived with the birthing chair. Mama and Noa got me settled in it. I clutched the arms and yelped.

My attention was drawn back to Adam when Dree asked again, "Where are people?" The carts sat silent.

"Around," Adam said, waving his arm toward the river.

"Bring here," Dree ordered.

"Emek," Adam said. Emek marched down the riverfront, beyond the barge dock. They had obviously prearranged this.

I found I could communicate with Dree, in pictures. I *sent* him images of me growing up in the colony, happy people, feasts, singing and dancing, people planting and harvesting crops. And I also *sent* images of Cray helping us.

After a particularly violent contraction, a thought came to me. There was a whole big continent on the southern part of this world. We didn't need much room, and could eventually expand into the mountains. Why not leave us here, and they could live down there. I *sent* a picture of it to Dree, and he presented it to the gatekeeper. I also *sent* a picture of people in the trees attacking carts. The violence of another contraction went with the image.

While Dree delivered my message, I got a *call* from Dela. Something about problems she couldn't handle.

'Not now. Having baby. Later.'

'I need help now.' I passed her to Mama. I was very busy.

"Push," Noa said. "I feel her crown." I screamed, and Marisa popped out. Noa wiped her off, wrapped her up, and handed her to me. The baby looked at me briefly, and went for the breast. I sat and panted as the afterbirth came out.

And then Mama screamed and I felt a different kind of pain. The gatekeepers had killed Uncle Adam.

Numb, I *reached* into the carts, *threw* the gatekeepers into the river, and shut everyone out. I closed my eyes and held on to my baby as if she were a life preserver.

I was dimly aware of being cleaned up and carried to a bed. I closed out everyone except my baby. All I wanted to do was hold Marisa and bond with her. This would become deeper than what Mama and I had.

#

The next day, when I came to myself, Charley told me it had been an accidental shot from a cart that hit Adam. The surviving alien was trying to contact us, but I was the only one who could *contact* him.

I took a deep breath and *reached* for Dree. There was a sense of safeness, and an image of our world, with only us in it. In another image I *saw* a picture of Harmony with a gatekeeper cart next to it. The cart faded out as it moved away. The Gatekeepers had given us our world. I sank back into my pillows. We had won. And lost.

I touched a delicate black curl on my baby's head. I had her to take care of now. I would grieve for Uncle Adam later.

The next day, Charley carried little Marisa and me down to join everyone else from the colony to see Uncle Adam off.

Gabe met us and led us to the barge dock. "It's up to us now," he told me. I sensed the emptiness within him, and gave him a mental hug. The rest of Adam's children were huddled around Kareth, whose face looked empty and flat.

Emek and his son Gan stood tall and solemn. Emek was the leader now.

Mama had the grimmest face I'd ever see on her, red eyes and clenched teeth. Only when she saw me and Marisa, did she relax a bit.

"Say hi to Gramma," I said. Marisa waved a tiny arm. Mama looked at the baby and turned to Papa, who drew her into his arms.

Soon, I found that Marisa knew what I knew, even though she had no way to express it yet. It was as if I'd grown a new Talent, one I could work with and enjoy.

List of characters

Perri – at sixteen, her Talent is more than she can handle.
Peter, her twin brother.

From Earth:
Lyn, their mother
Larry, Lyn's cousin, best friend, and mate
Doc Richard, Lyn's eldest cousin
      Alice, his wife, a nurse
Bay, Doc's nephew
      Pauli, Bay's mate, Lyn's niece
      Charley, their eldest son
      Beth, their eldest daughter
Art, Bay's cousin, a scientist
      Betty, his wife
      Art, Jr., their eldest son
      Joan, their eldest daughter
Chad, Bay's cousin
Maria, Bay's sister and Chad's mate
      Anne, their eldest daughter and Peter's mate to be
Bill, Lyn's nephew
Allen, Lyn's nephew

From Ruthor:
      Adam, Lyn's half-brother
            Gabriel (Gabe), his eldest son
            Han, his second son
            Amy, his eldest daughter

Bramites:
Kareth, Adam's mate
Emek, their leader and direct descendent of Prophet Bram
Noa, head medic

      Karil, her mate
Tara, Kareth's mother

Treesa
Barad, her mate
Neela and Cam, who started it all
Many others

Wati:

      Judee, matriarch and friend of Lyn
      Dela, her second daughter
      Hori, her third daughter

Cray, of Onan
Dree of Onan
The Gatekeepers
Other aliens